_A_ CANDLELIGHT ROMANCE

CANDLELIGHT ROMANCES

The Fateful Promise, LORENA ANN OLMSTED
Laurie's Legacy, JACQUELYN AEBY
The Lost Inheritance, ISABEL CABOT
Midsummer Eve, LOUISE BERGSTROM
The Reluctant Heart, ARLENE HALE
Strange Exile, LAURA SAUNDERS
Evil Island, JENNIFER BLAIR
The Secret Challenger, ANNIE L. GELSTHORPE
Designs on Love, GAIL EVERETT
The First Waltz, JANET LOUISE ROBERTS
Tender Harvest, ARLENE HALE
The House of the Golden Dogs, LOUISE BERGSTROM
Pattern of Loving, CHRISTINA ABBEY
The Pink Camellia, LOUISE BERGSTROM
House at River's Bend, RUBY JENSEN
Be My Love, ARLENE HALE
Companion to Danger, JACQUELYN AEBY
Time for Trusting, CHRISTINA ABBEY
House of Cain, SUZANNE ROBERTS
Three Silver Birches, RUTH MCCARTHY SEARS
Stranger at the Gate, LYNN WILLIAMS
Harvest of Years, MARY FORKER FORD
Terror at Tansey Hill, SUZANNE ROBERTS
Kanesbrake, JENNIFER BLAIR
The Divided Heart, ARLENE HALE
Dangerous Yesterdays, ARLENE HALE
Midnight Nightmare, ARLENE HALE
Perilous Weekend, ARLENE HALE
The Moonlight Gondola, JANETTE RADCLIFFE
Serena, JACQUELYN AEBY
The Encounter, RUTH MCCARTHY SEARS
Diary of Danger, JACQUELYN AEBY
House of the Sphinx, LOUISE BERGSTROM
The Trillium Cup, JACQUELYN AEBY
The Secret of the Priory, SOFI O'BRYAN
The Bride of Belvale, HARRIET RICH
Dangerous Assignment, JENNIFER BLAIR
Walk a Dark Road, LYNN WILLIAMS
False for a Season, JACQUELYN AEBY
The Gentleman Pirate, JANETTE RADCLIFFE
Tower in the Forest, ETHEL HAMILL
The Golden Falcon, BETTY HALE HYATT

Quest for
Alexis

by

Nancy Buckingham

A CANDLELIGHT ROMANCE

Published by
DELL PUBLISHING CO., INC.
1 Dag Hammarskjold Plaza
New York, New York 10017

Chapter One

As I turned the corner of Madison Avenue and Forty-second Street, I faced a bitter wind blowing across town. A scatter of snowflakes whirled by, stinging my cheeks. I shivered, hunching deeper into my coat. I'd planned to use my lunch hour choosing a cocktail dress for a party the agency was throwing, but the icy wind changed my mind. Tomorrow would have to do.

I dived into the nearest lunch counter and ordered coffee and a corned beef sandwich. It seemed that everyone in Manhattan had the same idea. The place was crammed. But I squeezed in beside a weather-beaten little man who was wolfing a hot dog as if it was his first food in days. Idly, as I sat sipping my scalding coffee, I scanned his newspaper with him.

The front page screamed the usual political crisis. I hardly took in where it was this time and let my eye wander down the page to find something more interesting. A small headline caught and riveted my attention: EXILED CZECH PATRIOT MISSING.

In the stuffy overheated atmosphere I went cold with shock, feeling the blood drain from my face, my fingertips. The pounding of my heart throbbed in my ears. It had to be Alexis. What other Czech exile would rate a front-page mention? But I could see only the alarming headline, the story itself coming below the fold of the page.

"Please," I blurted out, "may I have a look at your paper for a minute?"

The little man stared at me in astonishment. Then, stuffing the last piece of hot dog into his mouth, he stood up and held out the newspaper.

"Keep it, lady! You're welcome."

My hands trembled, and I had to steady myself before I could focus on the print.

Alexis Karel . . . celebrated liberal writer . . . dedicated anti-Communist . . . vanished from his home in Sussex, England. The short paragraph added the information that Miss Belle Forsyth, the nurse who was employed by Dr. Karel to look after his invalid wife, was also missing. Police were investigating the mystery.

I dropped the paper and stared blindly into the steamed-up mirror behind the counter. The story was unbelievable, fantastic. It didn't even begin to make sense in my numbed mind.

All at once I jerked into action. I had to get out of this place; I had to be doing something. I slid off the stool, tripping in my haste so that I nearly fell. As I emerged into the street, I felt the sudden slap of ice-cold air. Without any clear plan in mind, I broke into a run and didn't stop running until I arrived back at the Madison Avenue offices of Brand, Feiffer, and Coles. On the eighth floor, I stepped out of the elevator and walked smack into the solid frame of Hugo Blair, the copy chief and my immediate boss.

Hugo took the impact calmly, holding me pinned against him.

"Gail, baby! Take it easy."

"It's terrible, Hugo," I gasped. "Look what I've just seen in the paper."

He released me and read the paragraph where I stabbed my finger urgently.

"Alexis Karel! Isn't he the guy who's your uncle? The one who took care of you after your parents died?"

I nodded miserably. "What can it mean, Hugo—saying that he's *vanished?* I've got to know what it's all about. I'll have to telephone home to England and find out exactly what has happened."

"Sure, you do that, Gail. There might be some further news by now."

He walked with me down the corridor into the large room he and I shared with the other copywriters. Two of the men were there, working on rush jobs, and hardly glanced up. The others were all out to lunch. Hugo pushed me into a chair and picked up the phone on his desk.

"Tell me the number, Gail, and I'll put the call through."

Hugo was completely unflappable, always remaining cool even amid the permanent hysteria of the advertising world. It was the thing that had first struck me about him, the thing that had first made me like him so much.

"Yes, Sussex, *England*," he repeated to the switchboard girl. "And hurry it up, Maisie, will you?" Leaning forward, he touched my arm. "Who do you want to talk to, Gail? Your aunt?"

I shook my head in a daze. Poor Madeleine! I just couldn't bear to think what she must be going through at this moment. After her long ordeal in Czechoslovakia, she had no reserves of strength left to cope with a shock like this.

"No, I'd better not speak to Madeleine," I said. "Not until I've had a word with Rudi. He's my uncle's secretary. He'll know as much as anyone."

Hugo gave me a brief, compassionate smile. "Try not to worry, Gail. It may all be cleared up by now."

I sat there on the edge of my chair nervously, and when the phone rang I leaped to my feet. Hugo picked it up, asking, "Who's that speaking?" Then to me he said, "It's the man you want."

"Rudi! It's me—Gail!" My voice was choked and tight. "I just read about Alexis in the paper. For God's sake, what's happened?"

"Gail!" His astonishment was obvious. "I . . . I suppose I should have let you know at once. But there was nothing you could do, and I didn't want to worry you. It's a terrible business."

"It hardly said anything in the paper, Rudi," I cut in. "Just that Alexis has vanished and the police are investigating. What's it all about?"

"I wish I could tell you, Gail. I wish I knew. But we have no idea what happened, or where they might be." There was a pause, and I sensed Rudi's reluctance. "Did you know . . . did the newspaper mention that Belle is missing also?"

"Yes, I read that. But what does it mean? I don't understand."

It was easy to call to mind a picture of Belle Forsyth. She was the sort of woman who makes a swift and lasting impression—tall and graceful in her movements, with gorgeous copper-colored hair which she wore sleekly coiled on the crown of her head. I remembered Alexis saying it was a miracle to have found someone so eminently suitable. A trained nurse, but, more important, a charming companion for Madeleine, quiet and never fussy, accepting my aunt's unpredictable moods with patient tolerance. When the chance had come for me to work for six months at my firm's head office in New York, I had been able to accept with an easy conscience, knowing that Madeleine would have the best of care.

Rudi was saying, "The last I saw of Alexis was two nights ago when he went up to bed. Everything seemed perfectly normal, and he was talking of making an early start on the proofs of his book. So when he hadn't appeared by eight-thirty yesterday morning, I went up to give him a call. But he was not in his bedroom. Then I realized that I'd not seen or heard anything of Belle, either, and the house was oddly quiet. I went to your aunt's room, thinking perhaps they were in there with her for some reason. But Madeleine was fast asleep, and I didn't like to wake her. After that, I searched high and low, and when I went over to the garage I found that the car was gone. I called next door to ask Sir Ralph and Lady Caterina, but they knew nothing. We all felt very worried. The whole morning we kept on hoping that Alexis and Belle would turn up with some simple explanation, but the time went on and on. By afternoon Sir Ralph said we ought to notify the police. They've been here ever since asking questions—and now the MI-Five people."

"What about Madeleine?" I asked fearfully. "How has she taken it?"

"She doesn't really know what's happened, Gail. I

mean, she doesn't realize that there's anything wrong."

"*What!*"

"Well, you see, she didn't wake up till midmorning, and by then it was obvious that something was seriously the matter. Sir Ralph and Lady Caterina agreed with me that the shock might have a terrible effect on Madeleine, so we quickly thought up some vague story about Alexis having to go off on urgent business and Belle being called away because a friend was ill. Fortunately, she seems to have accepted it—for the present."

In the circumstances, I thought, perhaps it was as well that my poor aunt was so innocently trusting, her mind quite without the normal suspicions of a logically thinking person. Alexis had never before gone off at a moment's notice and would certainly not have done so without telling Madeleine himself. And as for Belle, she'd always seemed to be without any family or close friends, so it would take a lot of believing that she had left my aunt stranded to go rushing off to someone else's bedside.

I sighed. "At any rate it's a relief to know that Sir Ralph and Lady Caterina are at Deer's Leap. They're so often away at this time of year."

"Yes, it's a lucky thing. Lady Caterina has been wonderfully good to Madeleine."

I should explain that my uncle and aunt lived in a self-contained wing of the sixteenth-century manor house which was the family home of Sir Ralph Warrender. He and his second wife, Caterina, who had been a prima donna at La Scala, were delightful people, kindly and generous. In time of trouble like this it would be impossible to have better friends.

Rudi cleared his throat. "Gail . . . I'm afraid for Alexis. Do you think . . . ?"

The fear in his voice released my own stifled terror. I caught my breath and felt the skin tighten at the nape of my neck. I could not put a precise name to what it was we both feared—unknown, faceless figures, working in the shadows. Russian or Czech or

British—the nationality was irrelevant, but all of them united in fanatical allegiance to the cause that Alexis had spent his lifetime denouncing.

Their reach was long and powerful. No exile, in whichever country had given him refuge, could ever feel completely safe. He and his family would always be at risk. Even outsiders could be swept into the net because, innocently, they knew too much. Had these ruthless people come for Alexis, I thought desperately, and had Belle Forsyth somehow interrupted them?

Suddenly I couldn't bear to be three thousand miles from Madeleine. I wanted to be with her. I *had* to be with her.

"Rudi, I'm coming home. The very first flight I can get."

"But Gail!" he protested. "It's such a long way and you have your job to think of . . ."

"I can't help it about my job at a time like this. The firm will have to understand that I've got to get home right away."

Hugo gave me an encouraging nod and at once reached for a telephone on another desk. I guessed what he was doing. Finding me a London flight. Then, afterward, he would fix it with the boss. Dear, thoughtful Hugo!

Rudi still seemed doubtful. "I don't know what to say, Gail. Of course it would be an enormous help having you here, but I don't want you to think that you *have* to come. I can manage. In fact, I've arranged for an agency nurse to start tomorrow morning."

"An agency nurse!" I exclaimed. "A stranger! Madeleine will hate that."

"Don't forget that Lady Caterina is only next door. But it didn't seem fair to expect her to do too much. I thought I ought to get someone else in. . . . Gail, I promise to keep in touch so that you'll know at once what develops."

I realized that poor Rudi felt partly to blame, as if he'd failed us all by not preventing this dreadful thing from happening.

Rudi Bruckner had been with Alexis for two years

now. As a leader of student resistance in Prague in 1968 he had become a hunted man, a perpetual risk to his friends and to the married sister who had brought him up. Eventually, like so many others, like Alexis himself, Rudi had been smuggled across the border into freedom. Like so many others, too, he had arrived on Alexis Karel's doorstep with just the clothes he stood in and a letter of introduction.

Normally, Rudi would have stayed at Deer's Leap only until such time as Alexis's refugee contacts in England could find him a home, a suitable job. But Rudi had begged not to be sent away. He had proved to be an invaluable secretary for Alexis, and Madeleine had taken to him from the start. He was always wonderfully patient and understanding with her.

"Rudi," I said gently, "you mustn't blame yourself for what's happened."

"But, Gail, you don't understand." His voice was intolerably sad.

"Yes, I think I do understand. And I'm sure there was nothing you could have done to prevent it."

He said heavily, "I keep going over things in my mind, Gail. Was there something I missed, some disturbance in the night, *anything?* The trouble is, I seem to sleep so heavily. Why didn't I even hear the car driving away?"

"You wouldn't, not from the garage."

I broke off, because Hugo had raised a finger to catch my attention. He whispered, "You're on an evening flight. London Airport ten A.M."

I nodded at him gratefully. "Listen, Rudi, I'm coming home tonight. Be with you sometime tomorrow midday. See you then."

Putting down the phone, I sat back in my chair and stared at Hugo bleakly.

He frowned. "It didn't sound as if that guy could do much to fill you in, Gail. What did he have to say?"

As briefly as possible I repeated what Rudi had told me. "He hasn't any more idea what it's all about than I have. It seems a complete mystery."

Hugo hesitated, giving me a look that was unusual-

ly diffident for him. "This nurse of your aunt's—Belle
Forsyth. What's she like? Young?"

"About twenty-seven or twenty-eight, I'd guess.
Why?"

"Attractive?"

"Yes, very." Then his meaning hit me. "Hugo, you
aren't suggesting . . . ?"

"It's the obvious answer, isn't it? Both of them missing at the same time—and your aunt a permanent invalid. Of course, the paper doesn't say so straight out.
But obviously that's what you're meant to think, all
right."

I was so choked with outrage that I could hardly
speak. "If . . . if you knew Alexis, you'd never dream
of suggesting such a horrible thing. He's absolutely
devoted to Madeleine."

"But he's a man, Gail. And the right sort of age for
jumping the tracks. What is he . . . fifty?"

"Forty-nine," I whispered.

Hugo nodded thoughtfully. "I can see how you don't
like to think it of your uncle. But consider the alterna-
tives. That the Commies have got him . . . or that he's
defected and gone over to their side. Honestly, Gail,
when you come to think about it, isn't it better this
way?"

Chapter Two

Hugo drove me to Kennedy Airport.

The snow, after intermittent flurries all day, had
grown heavier when darkness fell, filling me with fore-
boding that I would never get away. I felt a great
sense of thankfulness when at last I heard my flight
number being called.

Saying goodbye to Hugo was hard when it came to
the point. We'd grown to be good friends in the four
months I'd been in New York, and now I didn't know
if I would ever see him again.

"I'm going to miss you, Hugo," I said.

He smiled down at me ruefully. "I'd hate us to lose touch, Gail. It's been great knowing you. You'll come back if you possibly can, won't you? We'll keep that desk dusted."

I stood on tiptoe and kissed him. "Thanks, Hugo. Thanks for everything." There was a lump in my throat as I turned away.

The plane was only half full, and I had no one sitting next to me. I leaned back wearily, shutting my eyes and ears to everything around me. I could have done without taped music or films. The last few hours had been frenzied, packing my things and settling up with the two girls whose apartment I had shared, generally freeing myself of commitments. Now, for the first time since the news about Alexis had hit me, I was alone. I could think.

In all the dark mystery surrounding my uncle's disappearance there was one thing I was sure of, though it did little to comfort me. Hugo's interpretation, built upon the sly hint in the newspaper report, was completely and utterly wrong.

Alexis was an attractive, virile-looking man. Though his hair was prematurely white, it grew thickly from his wide brow, setting off the healthy tanned skin of his face—a man who could easily pass for ten years younger. But it was well known that Alexis Karel was tied to a frail and chronic invalid. Perhaps, to strangers, the conclusion was inevitable that he had become infatuated with his wife's beautiful young nurse, and they had run away together.

But I knew Alexis better than that. I was closer to him than anyone—apart from Madeleine herself.

My deep feelings of affection, of love, for Alexis went back to those early days in Prague, even before he became my uncle. Alexis and my father had been friends from the time of their first meeting, soon after Father was posted to the British Embassy there. It was a friendship that had led to trouble. The Czech government made clear their strong disapproval of foreign diplomats who showed partiality to critics of the re-

gime, and my father was discreetly recalled to London.
But shortly before this happened, Mother's younger
sister Madeleine came out to stay with us in Prague,
and there she met Alexis.

My mother often told me about it afterward, a story
that caught my romantic imagination as a child. "When
you fall deeply in love as they did," she said once,
smiling sadly to herself, "the differences of upbringing
and background seem so unimportant. Your father
and I could see what was happening from the very
beginning. We knew Madeleine and Alexis would be
married."

I remember how I hated it when we had to return
to London, leaving behind the uncle and aunt I'd
grown so fond of. At ten years old I could see no reason why they shouldn't come with us and tried to make
an issue of it.

"Don't be silly, Gail," said my mother in exaspera-
tion. "This is Uncle Alexis's country. He's a Czech
citizen, and his work is at the university in Prague."

So I switched my tactics. "Well, why can't we stay
here? I like it here. I don't want to go back to London."

I wasn't told, then, of my father's mild disgrace—
not until I was older, by which time he had spent
three years or so in relatively minor jobs in London.
When at last it was considered that he had served a
suitable penance, he was sent to Japan. He and Mother
were flying to Tokyo, leaving me behind at boarding
school—and their plane crashed. My parents and the
other passengers were lost in an arctic wasteland five
hundred miles from Anchorage.

By then, Alexis and Madeleine had been living in
England for nearly twelve months.

In the intervening years, they had been through a
terrible time. Though feared and hated by the Novotny
regime, Alexis himself had been too popular a hero to
be attacked directly. So Madeleine was used as a
weapon against him, in a vicious game of cat-and-
mouse. She would be picked up for interrogation by
the secret police, sometimes for days at a time, returning from these sessions in a condition of dazed shock.

It was by such methods that they succeeded in silencing Alexis, until eventually friends in the underground movement managed to smuggle them both out of Czechoslovakia.

But for Madeleine, escape came too late. The mental anguish and physical hardship she suffered, the loss of her baby, born dead, had been more than my poor aunt could withstand. She was now a semi-invalid and would remain so for the rest of her life. She spent most of the time in her room, and often her withdrawal from reality was so complete it seemed impossible to get through to her.

It was Alexis who'd had to shoulder the whole burden of responsibility for their thirteen-year-old orphaned niece. One terrible day in early June, a day of sticky sweltering heat, he had arrived at my school to break the news of the death of my parents to me. I knew instantly from the look on his face, even before the headmistress left us alone together in her study.

"It's Mummy and Daddy, isn't it? Something happened."

Alexis took me by the shoulders, gently, his gray eyes looking gravely into mine. "Yes, Gail. You must be very brave. The plane crashed. There were no survivors."

He had driven me back with him to Deer's Leap, the beautiful, rambling old manor house deep in the Sussex weald where he and Madeleine now lived—thanks to the generosity of Sir Ralph Warrender.

Sir Ralph had been cultural attaché at the Embassy in Prague in the old days. He had not been unaware of what was happening to Madeleine and Alexis, though impotent to help. Sudden blindness had forced Sir Ralph to resign his post. He and Caterina had returned to England and retired to his family home. And when within a year Alexis had arrived in England too, an exile, Sir Ralph had at once stepped in with the offer of the west wing of his manor house as a refuge, as a retreat where Madeleine could spend her days in peace and tranquility.

In the weeks that I stayed at Deer's Leap before the

start of the next school term, a new relationship developed between Alexis and myself—more than just affectionate uncle and adoring niece. I clung to him as the pivot of my existence, the one person who could give meaning to my shattered life. But my feelings for Alexis were not in the least selfish. I always knew that Madeleine's welfare counted above everything else for him.

"Your poor aunt endured more than I can possibly tell you," he confided to me in those first few days. "A number of times I pleaded with her to leave Czechoslovakia and go back to England so that she would be safe. You see, marrying me had not deprived her of her British nationality, so it could have been arranged. But Madeleine refused to consider leaving the country if it meant leaving me." Alexis blinked away the tears that had come into his eyes and smiled at me. "And now, Gail, you and I will look after her together, won't we?"

We became, as it were, conspirators in caring for Madeleine, with an unspoken pact that she was to be sheltered and protected at all costs. Alexis was shrewd enough to understand, I think, that this intense concentration on someone else's needs was the best possible thing for me just then, helping me to overcome the grief I felt at my parents' death.

From then on Deer's Leap became my home, and I grew to love every mellow stone of it, every nook and moss-filled crevice. There was a timeless quality about the ancient manor, as if its very fabric had grown out of the sandy heath upon which it stood. The grounds, except for some hard-won lawns and rock gardens just around the house and terrace, defied all attempts at taming with domestic plants. It was a lovely wilderness of bracken and heather, with dense encroaching clumps of wild rhododendron and quiet woodland glades where a spotted fallow deer could now and then be glimpsed. A wonderful playground for a solitary, imaginative child. I loved the lake, where I swam when it was warm, and used to spend hours drifting in the dinghy while I read a book or just lay back in dreamy contemplation, waiting for a kingfisher to swoop down from the conifers and pluck a small trout from the water.

And after I left school and was working in London, Deer's Leap was still the place I loved to be above all others. Most weekends when I could get away I would drive down to Sussex. If the offer of a six-month spell at BFC's New York office had come at some other time, I might even have turned it down. But when it did come, it seemed like a deliverance from Brett Warrender.

It was at Deer's Leap that I met Brett again for the first time since I was a child. I had known him before in Czechoslovakia, known and disliked him with single-minded intensity.

Brett had spent much of the long vacation—he was at Cambridge then—visiting his father in Prague just after Sir Ralph had married Caterina. Since both of us were the offspring of Embassy officials, it was inevitable that our paths should cross now and again.

At first I had approved of Brett enormously, because he spoke to me in such a friendly, natural way, with no hint of condescension despite his nineteen years to my ten. But I gathered, from an amused remark tossed across the luncheon table, that "young Brett" wasn't backward and knew his way around with women. And it wasn't long before I received humiliating proof of that.

We were in an anteroom at the Embassy one afternoon, deep in an absorbing discussion—Brett doing the talking and me a rapt listener—about the new wave of Czech film directors.

"Men like Mrynych and Milos Forman have a completely fresh approach to the problem of . . ." He broke off as the door behind me opened. It was Eileen Peters, an Embassy secretary. Eileen had ash-blond hair and long shapely legs—and instantly she was the target of all Brett's attention.

"Oh, I was looking for your father," she said with a coy little laugh.

Brett awarded her a dazzling smile. "Won't I do instead?"

"Well, that depends."

I was totally forgotten. Wretchedly, I crept out of the room, and I doubt that Brett even noticed my going.

I might have forgiven him this once, but a few days later it happened again, with some other girl. I was furious. I was madly jealous. I vowed I would hate and despise Brett Warrender forever.

And nothing in the intervening years had caused me to change my opinion. On getting his honors degree, Brett had rebelled against going into the diplomatic service like his father. Instead, he had spent two or three years roaming the world doing his own thing before eventually landing a job as a TV man-on-the-spot reporter. This proved to be just his *métier,* and Brett rapidly became one of the small screen's best-known faces.

By a strange combination of circumstances, we had never met in all this while, even though I was at Deer's Leap so often. Brett spent a great deal of his time abroad. When he did come home to visit his father and stepmother, it just so happened that I had always missed seeing him.

Now and then I'd watched Brett on TV, and these programs only confirmed my preformed judgment of him. An overconfident man, an arrogant man—too aware of his own ability, far too aware of his attractiveness to women.

So when I arrived at Deer's Leap one Saturday for the weekend, it was with mixed feelings that I learned we had all been invited to dine with the Warrenders because Brett would be at home.

"We were working it out," said Alexis. "You two haven't met each other since that summer in Prague, have you?"

At least it would be interesting, I told myself, actually to see him in the flesh after all this time.

At seven-thirty Alexis, Madeleine, Rudi, and I trooped through the doorway that divided the two parts of the house, a door that was always left unlocked, though seldom used unless by invitation.

The Warrenders were in their drawing room—the beautiful Ivory Room that had always fascinated me, filling me with wonder at the hours of dedicated craftmanship that had gone into the carving of those fragile treasures. The two men rose to their feet to greet us, and Sir Ralph held out his hand to me, smiling the unseeing smile of a blind man.

"Gail, my dear, you are always welcome. And this evening doubly so. My son has been looking forward to seeing you again."

I turned to Brett, and our eyes met. Until the day I die, I shall be able to recall the exact quality and texture of that moment. The sudden tensing of my heart muscles, the feeling of panic, of struggling for breath, the lost, despairing sensation that I was drowning.

From the sofa by the fire, Caterina gave her musical laugh. "Well, Brett, what do you say? Gail is no longer a shy little schoolgirl, is she?"

He grinned at his stepmother affectionately. "I hate to contradict you, Caterina, but I deny that Gail was ever shy. An intelligent and fascinating child, as I recall—when she wasn't sulking."

It was almost a relief to find that Brett could still infuriate me.

Over dinner it emerged that Brett was now in a position to pick and choose his assignments. In the future, it was unlikely that he would need to spend so much of his time abroad. "We hope we shall be seeing a great deal more of him from now on," his father told us.

Across the table I met Brett's eyes again and read the challenging message in them. I glanced away hastily, disturbed and confused. By the end of the evening I felt strangely tired, almost exhausted, as if I had been under an unbearable strain.

Next morning at breakfast Alexis asked me casually, "What did you think of Brett?"

The shattering effect of his personality was still upon me. But I fought against it. "He has a high opinion of himself, I'd say."

"With good reason," said Alexis mildly. "Brett has a clever mind, and his analysis of a political situation is very acute."

I gave a casual shrug. "Oh, well, I doubt that I'll be joining his fan club."

On Monday morning Brett called me at the Mayfair offices of Brand, Feiffer, and Coles. He came to the point without any preamble.

"Gail, you must have dinner with me tonight."

The curious feeling of panic gripped me again, but it didn't even occur to me to refuse or invent some excuse. I knew when I was defeated. I just said, "Yes, of course."

"I'll pick you up at your place at seven-thirty—okay? And by the way, Gail, keep the rest of the week free. I've a feeling we'll want to see a lot of each other from now on."

And we did. Too much, perhaps. Our relationship was too intense, too urgent, too demanding. Looking back, I think I was never truly happy. I felt so unsure of Brett, and each time I saw him I dreaded that this might be the last time. I knew jealousy such as I had never experienced with any other man. He made me angry, and we often quarreled, so that I lived always on the edge of despair. But the times when everything was good between us seemed to make up for all the rest.

And then, suddenly, with the spring, it was over.

I still went down to Deer's Leap quite often on weekends, but Brett kept clear when I was there. He accepted a couple of assignments abroad that took him away for most of the summer. Alexis, with his usual tact, didn't press me for details, and I made no attempt to explain. For all our closeness, this was something too painful to be talked about.

It was in the autumn that Alexis told me about the plans for a documentary on his life and work.

"You mean *Brett* is going to make it?" I exclaimed, horrified. "But why Brett? Why does it have to be him?"

Alexis gave me a brief, pitying smile.

"It's almost an honor, really. Brett is a top name in

television nowadays, and of course he's known me for so long that he understands the way I think. For myself, I couldn't be more pleased." My uncle regarded me intently. "You see, my dear, Brett Warrender's stamp on the film will help it make a big impact, and I want all the publicity I can get at the moment. It will help achieve a widespread sale for my book."

Alexis didn't need to explain to me that he wasn't concerned about the money involved, except insofar as it would allow him to give further aid to his refugees. This new book took the lid off a great deal that the Communists would have liked to keep hidden about the Stalinist trials of the 1950s.

"Men like Clementis and Slansky were hanged, Gail, in order to terrify the whole nation and keep it subdued. The methods they used to extract false confessions—the methods they used on innocent people like poor Madeleine—these things need to be told. They have never been properly understood in the West. This is my chance to *make* them understood."

I supported my uncle all the way, of course, but still I felt dismayed that Brett should be the one to make the film that was to tie in with his book.

Alexis went on, "Brett and his production team will be in and out of Deer's Leap for quite some time." He ran his fingers through his thick white hair, a sign of nervousness. "I don't mind admitting that I've had great hopes, Gail. Perhaps, seeing a lot of each other again, you will be able to be friends once more. Who knows, you might even—"

I cut in quickly, my pride at stake. "I'm afraid I'm likely to be very busy myself in the next few months. I doubt if I'll be able to get down here very often."

I would have been hard put to it to find excuses for skulking in my Bayswater apartment every weekend. But fate decided to be kind. Only a week later Tom Grant, the London boss of Brand, Feiffer, and Coles, sent for me.

"How would you like to do a stint in the New York office, Gail? They've suggested an exchange of staff to compare our working methods."

It seemed the perfect answer to my problem. Moreover, it sounded exciting, a challenge, something to give me a new interest and break free from the state of dull apathy I'd been living in these past months.

"Great!" I said. "Count me in!"

Tom Grant raised his thick eyebrows and grinned. "Can you really say yes just like that? You amaze me, Gail. Haven't you any . . . male entanglements at the moment?"

"No entanglements," I said firmly.

In New York, I received regular progress reports from Alexis on the film-making. He was very happy about it and full of praise for Brett. He also made constant references to Elspeth Vane, the film's producer. A charming woman, he wrote, intelligent and talented as well as beautiful.

Alexis clearly had no idea that he was twisting a knife in my heart.

I was infinitely thankful for the lucky chance that had removed me from Deer's Leap at this time. And I guessed that Brett was equally thankful not to have me around. A break like ours must be clean-cut. Final.

The plane descended out of the murky sky and landed at London Airport a frustrating two hours late. There was no snow here, not even the threat of it. The air was raw as only English air can be, laden with a cold penetrating dampness. I was in no mood to waste time on airport buses and trains. Extravagantly, I hired a car to take me all the way to Deer's Leap.

There was a sad, lost look of winter upon the countryside, a veil of creeping mist dimming the starkness of bare fields. It didn't help my feeling of desolation.

At last we left the main roads behind and slipped through the deserted Sussex lanes, high-banked with crumbly sandstone. Leafless oak and elm trees arched overhead.

"It's just along here on the right," I told the driver as we crested the last rise. "You'll see the gateposts in a second."

He braked and swung between the tall stone pillars,

each capped with a delicately sculpted leaping deer. Gravel crunched wetly under the tires as we swept up the drive, and the sodden rhododendron bushes rose on either side, dark and impenetrable.

There were already a couple of cars on the fore-court, drawn up by the Gothic-arched porch that was the main entrance, the entrance used by the Warren-ders. The house was L-shaped, and the west wing formed the leg, with its own front door. I told the driver to stop there. The moment I had paid him he shot off again, leaving me standing beside my cases. I lingered for a few moments, staring up at Deer's Leap.

Every outline, every feature was blurred by the clammy mist. The pointed gables and twisted chimney stacks, the tall mullioned windows with their diamond leaded panes. Where it showed behind the clinging ivy, the time-worn stonework was dark with damp. But even like this, at its most uninviting, I still loved the old house.

Picking up my cases, I turned toward the door. Just as I got there it opened and a stranger came out. Rudi was right behind him, standing in the doorway. His eyes flashed me a warning look.

"Ah . . . good afternoon," he greeted me in a formal voice. "I heard the car arriving. I'll be with you in just a moment." He returned his attention to the man. "I'm sorry I can't give you any further information, but there it is."

The man, huddled in a short tweed overcoat, nodded to Rudi, flicked me a casual glance, and walked off toward one of the cars. We went inside and Rudi closed the door behind us.

"I'm sorry to have sounded so unwelcoming, Gail. But that was a reporter and I didn't want him to guess who you were."

A shiver ran through me. "A reporter? Have they discovered anything, Rudi? Is there any news?"

His deep-set dark eyes, usually so alive when they looked at me, were clouded with distress.

"So you haven't seen a newspaper since you landed?"

"No, I didn't stop to . . ." My heart began to thud, and I felt suddenly queasy. "Rudi, what is it?"

He hesitated, then said reluctantly. "The news came through this morning. Alexis had been seen, Gail."

"Seen! What does that mean? Where has he been seen?"

"In Majorca. Alexis is in Majorca, staying at some luxury hotel. Belle Forsyth is with him."

Chapter Three

My first reaction was blind fury. Why did people suggest such foul things, even people I was fond of? Hugo could be forgiven; he didn't know Alexis. But there was no excuse for Rudi. He had worked with Alexis for the past two years and more than any other man alive had reason to understand the depth of my uncle's idealism, his burning sincerity.

I said fiercely, "You know that isn't true! You know Alexis has never even looked at another woman, let alone . . ."

Rudi made a hopeless little gesture with his hands. "Do you think it pleases me to say it, Gail? I'm only passing on what was reported on the radio."

"You really believe this story, don't you?" I said, staring at him incredulously.

Rudi took me by the shoulders, holding me gently. "Gail, my dear . . . I feel torn apart by this news. Shattered. But I have to believe it."

"Just on the strength of a garbled story by a newspaper reporter who was trying to impress his editor!"

"It was an official news-agency report," he said in a quiet, flat voice. "And it was quoted as fact by the BBC. There is the car, too. It has been found abandoned at London Airport. I've arranged to have it brought home."

I was stabbed with sudden fear. "What about Madeleine? Have you said anything to her about this?"

"No, she still knows nothing. When I told Sir Ralph and Lady Caterina that you were coming home, they agreed it was best to leave it to you to decide what Madeleine was to be told."

I nodded. "How have *they* taken the news?"

"Well, of course . . . Sir Ralph is very kind, but it's been a terrible shock to him."

"You mean he believes it, too?" I said bleakly.

Rudi didn't answer, but just looked at me with sadness in his eyes.

So far I'd given no thought to the Warrenders and the effect on them. Inevitably, as the owners of Deer's Leap, they were caught up in this sudden blaze of publicity, and I knew how much Sir Ralph must be hating it. He had very rigid views about what was right and what was wrong, and he disliked scandal of any kind. Besides, as the man who had helped Alexis after his escape from Czechoslovakia, Sir Ralph would feel himself betrayed—if this horrible story were true.

Somehow, I had to make them understand that it *wasn't* true. That it *couldn't* be true.

"I'd better go through and see Sir Ralph and Caterina right away," I said. "I've got to talk to them."

"Wait!" Rudi glanced at his wrist watch. "There's another news bulletin due in a couple of minutes. You ought to hear it."

I slipped out of my coat and dropped it on a chair before following him into the Oak Room, which Alexis used as his study. Like the hall, it seemed dismal in the failing afternoon light, the linenfold paneling lacking its usual warm polished gleam. The room was small, workmanlike, one wall lined with bookshelves. On the library desk Rudi had left a transistor radio. He switched it on, and the burst of pop music sounded incongruous in these surroundings. There was a time check, and then the smooth, unemotional voice of the BBC newscaster. The item about Alexis came fourth, after a bank holdup in Edinburgh.

Dr. Alexis Karel, about whom there has been some anxiety since he was reported missing from his Sussex home, has now been found to be safe and well at a

fashionable hotel in Palma, Majorca. Listeners were reminded that Dr. Karel was shortly to publish an important new book, *Czechoslovakia in Chains,* for
which it was understood he had received a large sum
for newspaper serialization in England and America.
Almost as an afterthought it was added that Miss Belle
Forsyth, who had been employed by Dr. Karel as his
invalid wife's nurse and companion, was staying at the
same hotel.

Rudi reached out and switched off the radio. I felt
too sickened to speak, and into the unhappy silence
the telephone rang, a sudden jarring noise.

"It's sure to be another newspaper," said Rudi.
"They haven't left us alone."

"Oh . . . will you answer it, then? I'll go and see the
Warrenders." I hesitated. "Is . . . is Brett at home?"

"No, he's not there now. He went back to London
yesterday." Picking up the phone, Rudi looked at me
sadly, and I realized that he had misinterpreted my
question. He believed that I was turning to Brett for
help—not that I wanted above everything to avoid him.
But somehow I couldn't bring myself to explain.

I went through the doorway that separated the west
wing from the main part of the house with a feeling of
apprehension. What was my reception going to be?

I hesitated in the staircase hall. It was quiet and dim
there, little light piercing the tall oriel window on this
dark winter afternoon. The great Elizabethan stairs
turned upward into shadow.

A studded door beside the stairway opened, and the
Warrenders' maid appeared, wheeling a tea cart. She
gave me her usual bright smile, then her face sobered.

"Hello, Miss Fleming. I heard you were coming."

"Hello, Jenny. Are Sir Ralph and Lady Caterina
alone?"

"Yes, I'm just taking in their tea."

She went to the door of the Ivory Room, obviously
expecting me to follow her in. But I hung back nervously.

"Jenny, tell them I'm here first, will you?"

"Yes, if you like."

A moment later I heard Caterina's exclamation, and she came hastening out to me. She was a generously built woman, an opera singer in the old tradition, yet as light on her feet as a dancer. Caterina was given to wearing long flowing garments in gorgeous fabrics, which invested her with regal dignity. Today, she was neck to ankles in a crimson velvet caftan.

"Gail, my poor little one—what a terrible, terrible business this is!" Impulsively, she hugged me and kissed my cheek, then drew me after her into the room, still voluble. "We've been so concerned, so worried. . . . Jenny, fetch another cup, please. Ralph, my darling, here she is, our poor dear Gail."

Her husband was standing before the hearth, with its superb ivory overmantel. He was a tall man with neatly parted iron-gray hair. In retirement, since his blindness, Sir Ralph had grown thinner, but he still held himself with an upright bearing. He stretched out his hand for me to take, but his welcome noticeably lacked the warmth of Caterina's.

"Good afternoon, Gail. You wasted no time coming back to England."

"I felt I had to come at once, Sir Ralph—for Madeleine's sake."

"Yes, poor soul. It's going to be an appalling shock to her, but she will have to know the truth."

The truth! He was taking it for granted that Alexis had cut loose from his responsibilities like a man without honor or principle. Even Caterina accepted it as a fact. For all her charm, for all her sincere concern for me, I could read the message in her large dark eyes. Alexis stood condemned!

I said quietly, stubbornly. "We can't be certain what the truth is, Sir Ralph. There must be some explanation. I know my uncle."

"I thought I knew him too, my dear. And so did a great many other people—tens of millions of them who admired and trusted and looked up to him." Sir Ralph sighed heavily. "It's bad enough in all conscience for any man to desert his wife and go off with some other woman. But for a man in Alexis Karel's position it's nothing less than criminal. Such a man has a duty he must never forget. His behavior must always be above reproach."

Sir Ralph broke off, and I saw that his face, vulnerable through blindness, was twitching with emotion. Caterina went quickly to him, taking his arm and coaxing him to sit down. She looked at me in a silent appeal not to upset her husband any further, and I realized that Sir Ralph had felt a deeper admiration for Alexis than I had ever guessed—an admiration that was now being shattered.

I said in a faltering voice, "I'm sorry. I can understand how you feel, but I can't believe it's . . . what it seems."

Tapping on the door, Jenny came in with the extra cup and saucer. Nobody spoke until she had left the room again. Then Caterina asked, "Have you seen Madeleine yet, Gail, my dear? She was so happy when I told her this morning that you were on the way home. I made up a little lie, I'm afraid—that you were coming for a holiday." She looked at me anxiously. "I did what I thought was for the best."

Sir Ralph cleared his throat. "It hasn't been easy to keep the news from reaching your aunt. If it weren't for her room being at the back of the house, it would have been impossible. We've been besieged here—a lot of damned newspaper reporters! And the police. We even had the security people sniffing around until this latest news came through."

"It must have been very unpleasant for you both. I'm truly sorry."

I watched Caterina as she drew the tea cart toward her and began to pour milk into the dainty china cups. Afternoon tea before the fire—it seemed to symbolize the lives of these two. A retired gentleman and his wife. Tranquility and comfort in gracious surroundings, the well-deserved reward for a lifetime's work. Some small recompense, perhaps, for the affliction of blindness.

Until two days before the Warrenders had been able

to count on this quiet, peaceful existence. But not any longer.

"If you don't mind," I said quickly, rising to my feet, "I think I'd better not stay for tea after all. I really must go up and see Madeleine. I would have done so before, only I wanted a word with you first."

Caterina's brow, usually so smooth beneath the crown of dark hair, was furrowed in distress.

"What will you say to your poor aunt, Gail? Will you tell her what has happened?"

"I don't know. I'll have to decide when I see how she is."

At the door I paused and glanced back at them. I couldn't shake off a curious sense of shame, as if I were the one to blame for this catastrophe.

It was up to me, somehow or other, to try and put things right. My decision was made in a flash, even as the thought entered my head.

"I'll go to Majorca," I announced. "I'm going to see Alexis and talk to him. Tomorrow!"

Caterina's eyes widened in astonishment. Sir Ralph frowned.

"I warn you, Gail," he said, "if you go rushing off after Alexis, you'll only be hurt. Badly hurt!"

Caterina hastily tried to soften her husband's words. "I beg you to consider, Gail, my dear one. It cannot be wise to act so impetuously."

"What else can I do?" I cried miserably. "I've got to do something. I can't just accept a thing like this as if it isn't important."

"Perhaps if you wait a little," she said without conviction, "Alexis will write and explain."

But I wasn't prepared to wait on the off chance of receiving a letter from Alexis. A letter was so one-sided! It couldn't be argued with, reasoned with. I was determined to see my uncle in the flesh, to talk to him face to face and demand an explanation.

Rudi heard me returning to the west wing and came out of the Oak Room to meet me.

"What did Sir Ralph have to say, Gail?"

"He believes it. And he blames Alexis—just as you do!"

"Be fair! I didn't say I *blamed* him, but it's no use shutting our eyes to what has happened."

"You don't *know* what's happened. I'd have thought that you of all people, Rudi, would stand up for Alexis, considering what he's done for you." My feeling of hurt bewilderment made me speak bitterly, unfairly. "Now I'm going up to see Madeleine."

My aunt's bedroom was a large apartment with a view over the terrace and tangled grounds to the ridge of heathland that in the mist was no more than a vague purplish haze. The lake was very calm, lying like a sheet of pale gray silk, fringed with the tall feathery spires of the fir trees.

Madeleine was seated by the window, an easel propped up before her, using the last of the fading light to catch the scene in one of her delicate watercolor paintings. I was relieved to see she was using watercolor today. When she painted in oils, her mood was very different. Angry and turbulent, the expression of a tortured mind. The results were often grotesque.

She heard the door click as I closed it and looked up. Rising swiftly to her feet, she held out her arms to me.

"Gail, darling! I didn't know you had arrived. Come and give me a kiss."

I went to her quickly and hugged her, putting my arms around her small, thin shoulders. For the moment I felt too choked with emotion to speak.

"It was a lovely surprise," she said happily, "when they told me you were coming home for a little holiday. Alexis has had to go away, did you know? But now, Gail, I shall have you for company."

I said huskily, "I'm afraid I have to go off again my-self tomorrow, just for a little while. It shouldn't be for very long."

She made a little moue of disappointment with her

lips. "Did Rudi tell you I have a new nurse? Just temporarily, you know. But I don't like her very much. She's not nearly as nice as Belle."

"I'm sorry about that, darling," I murmured.

She sighed. "Oh, well, it can't be helped. I expect they'll both be home soon—Alexis and Belle."

It shook me for a moment, hearing her link their names together. Had she some glimmering of what had happened, in spite of all that had been done to keep it from her? But looking searchingly into Madeleine's face, I felt sure that she knew nothing of the truth.

The truth! I was thinking just like the others, who were all so quick to condemn Alexis. In swift penance, I kissed my aunt's cheek a second time. "It's wonderful to see you, darling. You're looking so much better than when I went away."

My mother had often spoken of her younger sister as being very beautiful, and a pale ghost of this loveliness still lingered behind the marks of her ill-treatment at the hands of Novotny's secret police. The large golden eyes were sunk deep, and above her cheekbones the ivory skin was stretched like translucent parchment. Strangers tended to look away quickly, disturbed by the evidence of so much suffering. It was only those who knew her well and loved her who could be entirely natural in her presence. To me, Madeleine's face had a special quality. Despite all she had endured, there was still something that reminded me of my mother.

And now poor Madeleine was about to face even more suffering, worse than anything she had so far had to bear. How could I bring myself to break the news of Alexis's disappearance? How could I tell her that the husband she adored had apparently deserted her for another woman? Such a cruel, casually ruthless action was impossible to believe, and I didn't believe it. Not of Alexis!

While there was the slightest hope, I decided, the slimmest chance of an explanation that would clear everything up, it would be kindest to let Madeleine remain unknowing. I was going to see my uncle myself, and not until afterward would I tell Madeleine whatever it was she had to be told.

I stayed with her for half an hour, trying hard to make chatty conversation. I told Madeleine about New York, and she was interested because she had never visited America. Eventually, the temporary nurse appeared and announced in brisk professional tones that my aunt must rest.

"Mrs. Karel mustn't have too much excitement all at once," she said meaningfully.

Freda Aiken hadn't a trace of Belle's charm. She was a plain, dumpy woman in her mid-thirties, with frizzed hair and careless make-up. She gave me a look that made it clear she knew exactly what was going on and was relishing the spicy situation.

I stood up and smiled at Madeleine. "Yes, I mustn't overtire you, darling. I'll see you again later on."

As I was going downstairs I saw light spilling from the open door of the Winter Parlor and heard Rudi talking to someone. Then the other person spoke, and with a stab of alarm I recognized the voice.

Brett Warrender!

Chapter Four

I stood rigidly still, both hands clutching the banister rail for support. I wasn't prepared for this! I hadn't expected to come face to face with Brett without any warning. I'd thought he was in London, a safe distance away.

It was ten months since I'd last seen him, ten months since that evening in April when my jealousy had at last reached the snapping point. And Brett had faced me in a blaze of anger, denying nothing.

Of course I'd known that in coming to England, to Deer's Leap, the chances were that we should meet. Only I hadn't realized it would be like this. I hadn't imagined that just to hear Brett's voice would pitch me into such a turmoil of emotion.

I took several slow, deep breaths to steady myself. Then, after a moment, my legs still hesitant, I continued down the stairs and entered the room.

Brett's dark eyes met mine, and for a brief instant there was an acknowledgment of everything we had once meant to each other. But then the flash of intimacy was gone, and I was merely someone he happened to know rather well.

"Hello, Gail. They told me you were back. This is a hell of a mess, isn't it? I suppose you've been telling Madeleine. How did she take it?"

I shook my head. "I haven't told her. I couldn't."

"For heaven's sake! The longer you put it off, the worse it will be for her. There was some sense in keeping the news from Madeleine until you got home. But now that you're here, the sooner she knows the better. She's got to understand the sort of man Alexis has turned out to be!"

My anguish swiftly changed to anger. I forgot that Rudi was present and faced Brett furiously, seeing again his stubborn arrogance, his certainty that only he could be right.

"How dare you! It's not fair to judge Alexis without hearing his side."

"*His* side!" Brett's voice was scathing. "If you have any idea, Gail, that this will all blow over and you can save your uncle's Christlike image, you'd better forget it. That famous book of his which was all set to shake the world is a dead duck before it's even published. And so's the film I've been working on these past three months—a real PR job on Alexis Karel, saint and savior! It'll be so much useless junk now. The man's a laughingstock."

"Stop it!" I shouted. "I won't listen to you!"

"That was always your trouble, Gail. You never *would* listen. You just jump to conclusions."

"Isn't that exactly what you're doing about Alexis?"

"No, I'm merely facing facts. I suppose you realize that he's hopped it with the loot from his book. I gather he was paid a gigantic fee for the newspaper rights."

"Yes, and you know why, too! Alexis has always needed every penny he could scrape together to help his refugees. These people arrive here destitute and need to be put on their feet again and found somewhere to live. It all takes a great deal of money." I checked myself, knowing I was being tactless in front of Rudi.

"It's all right, Gail," he said quietly. "I haven't forgotten how much I owe Alexis Karel. And I never will—whatever is being said about him now, whatever may come to light. His life hasn't been easy, always having to worry more about others than about himself—and Belle is a very attractive woman." He glanced at Brett, then back at me, a desperate appeal for understanding in his eyes. "Is Alexis so much to blame for snatching at happiness?"

"There's just the little matter of deserting a wife who went through hell on his account," Brett pointed out viciously. "That's hardly going to endear him to the people who regarded him as a national hero. Not just Czechs but millions of people all over the world. People like my father."

"I feel dreadful about Sir Ralph," I admitted miserably. "I know how all this has upset him. But you're wrong, all of you, in what you think about Alexis. I don't believe he's gone off with Belle Forsyth—at least, not in the way you mean. There's some mistake, there must be—and I'm going to find out the truth."

"Such blind faith is touching," said Brett. "It's a pity you don't apply it to everyone."

Even now I was shocked to see the cold scorn in Brett's eyes. I had been imagining he was indifferent to me, but it was still war between us. Brett was making it clear there would be no forgiveness. No truce, even.

In the months since we parted, I had forgiven Brett a thousand times—and instantly hardened my heart once more. It had been so flagrant, his relationship with Elspeth Vane.

Brett had never denied the fact that they had been lovers; but it was nothing serious for either of them, he insisted, and over and done with before we met again, in England. Painful though it was to know about their love affair, I tried to accept the fact, to reconcile myself to it. To believe Brett when he told me it was a thing of the past. But unceasingly I was filled with terror that, compared to Elspeth Vane, he must find me naïve and ordinary.

Elspeth had so much to offer a man. She was tall and slender, with delicately molded features and raven black hair. As if such looks weren't enough for anyone to be blessed with, she was a career woman of exceptional ability. Within a very short time she had thrust to the top of the younger generation of television producers. Brett had admitted to me frankly that he would rather work with Elspeth than any other producer, male or female.

"She's brilliant, Gail," he said more than once. "She can grasp a vague idea of mine and translate it into crisp filmic terms. I admire her work enormously. But you don't have to worry, darling. To Elspeth, the job and . . . and her private life are two things apart. We work together now purely as colleagues. Honestly!"

I tried hard to believe him, to trust him completely. I fought to suppress the flushes of jealousy that swept me. But my constant feeling of inadequacy resulted in angry, bitter scenes. The final showdown between us was inevitable.

They had been making a TV film on Richard Cobden and the free-traders—Brett and Elspeth, the cameraman and the sound recordist who made up the team. They were due back in London one Friday after being up in Manchester for a couple of weeks, and Brett and I had a date for the same evening.

The previous evening I'd been working late, revising copy for the Sandalwood Cosmetics autumn campaign. As I stepped off the escalator at the Oxford Circus tube station, by sheer blind chance I bumped into Eddie Fox, the cameraman.

"Eddie, what are you doing back in town? I thought you weren't finishing in Manchester until tomorrow."

He grinned at me cheerfully. "We got through the

last few takes quicker than we expected, and Elspeth said we might as well pack it in and have a long weekend off."

My heart began to pound. Why on earth had I chosen this one evening to stay late at work? Brett might be at my apartment at this very moment, or trying to ring me! Calling a hasty goodbye to Eddie over my shoulder, I rushed onto the platform and just managed to jump on a train before the doors closed.

It was a long evening, waiting for Brett. As my phone stayed unbelievably silent, I lifted it several times to convince myself it was still working. At nine-thirty I dialed the number of Brett's apartment, but there was no answer.

Slowly, suspicion crawled into my mind. I suppose it had always been there, deep down, but at last I could fight it no longer. Hating myself for what I was doing, I rang the hotel in Manchester where the team had been staying.

"Is Mr. Brett Warrender there, please?"

The night clerk didn't hesitate. "Hold on, please, and I'll put you through to his room."

I heard a low-pitched buzz, a click, then a woman's voice, unmistakably Elspeth's voice. Cool, crisp, confident.

I was too numbed to say anything, and after a moment she began to get irritable. "Hello . . . who is it? There's something the matter with this damn phone, Brett!"

I heard him say, "Give it to me, then. Hello . . ."

As if it were an intricate action to perform, I put the phone back on its cradle. I don't remember going to bed that night, but I suppose I must have. Somehow, feeling drained and exhausted, I got myself to the office next day and pretended to work. In the evening, Brett came around to the apartment as if nothing in the world was wrong. He looked surprised at the state I was in.

"Darling, what's the matter?"

I had to force the words out because my throat was

tight and choked. "You stayed in Manchester last night!"

"That's right," he said easily. "I told you—remember?"

"But you finished filming a day early. I know that because I ran into Eddie."

Brett's face became a mask, giving nothing away. When he spoke, his voice was clipped and distant.

"We finished ahead of schedule, so the team came back to town. I stayed on overnight because an old boy who's some sort of descendant of Richard Cobden insisted on laying on a little dinner party. He'd been so helpful, digging out a lot of historical facts, that I could hardly refuse."

I said stingingly, "I notice you carefully avoided any mention of Elspeth!"

Brett stared at me, and a faint color crept into his face. After a long pause, he said heavily, "I didn't mention Elspeth because I knew how you'd react, Gail. I'm sick to death of this crazy jealousy of yours. It's completely insane!"

"Insane! I was insane ever to trust you!"

He threw back his head and laughed mirthlessly. "You've never trusted me for a single instant, Gail—not since I first told you about Elspeth. You're too damn possessive—that's your trouble. You resent every moment I'm not with you, every last second I'm not at your beck and call."

I went cold with fear at the storm I'd unleashed. I had never suspected this depth of resentment in Brett. Desperately, I wished I could go back, back to yesterday, to the time before my meeting with Eddie. I had been happy then, and I longed to wipe the past twenty-four hours from my mind.

Perhaps if Brett could convince me that I'd been wrong . . .

I said, "If . . . if you can give me your solemn word that you and Elspeth weren't . . . that you didn't . . ."

His face went dark. "No, I won't give you my solemn word! You can bloody well take me on trust, or we might as well finish. It's up to you!"

We were suddenly caught in a knot of silent fury, glowering at each other, hating each other. Confronting Brett, I felt pitifully small and vulnerable. I could only think of hitting back at him.

"All right then, we'll finish," I heard myself say in a shrill voice. "If that's the way you want it—goodbye!"

Turning my back on him, I stared out of the window, seeing nothing through the mist of my tears. Brett said my name softly. I stayed quite still, not looking round. A moment later he flung out of the room, slamming the door behind him. I heard his footsteps on the stairs, the street door closing. I heard his car start up and drive away, and it seemed as if Brett had abandoned me, wounded and bleeding.

Opposite, down on the pavement, some people were laughing.

Now, in a different room, a different time, we stared at each other and relived the bitterness of that last quarrel. Then, abruptly, Brett walked past me to the door.

"It's a waste of time trying to argue with you," he said. "My father tells me you have some idiotic plan to go rushing off to Majorca. What earthly good do you think that will do?"

"I have to go," I said. "To get at the truth."

"You know the truth, Gail, only you won't accept it. Don't be such a fool. Think of Madeleine and stay here."

"I *am* thinking of Madeleine," I cried. "You don't imagine I want to leave her at a time like this, for goodness sake! But I must, can't you see?"

Brett stood in the doorway, looking back at me. His eyes were cold, his mouth set in a hard straight line.

"If you're really determined to go, Gail," he said at last, "then I'll come with you."

Beside me, Rudi couldn't have been more astonished than I was myself. Brett didn't wait for me to answer but walked out into the hall, remarking over his shoulder, "You'd better let me know what you decide."

Rudi turned to me and said uneasily, "He was telling me, just before you came downstairs, about your plan to go to Majorca. Is it wise, Gail? I don't see what you can hope to achieve."

"What can I hope to achieve by doing nothing? At least I shall have done my best. I'm going, Rudi—I've made up my mind. Don't try and argue me out of it, *please*."

"Brett means what he says, you know. If you insist on going, he'll go with you."

"No, I won't let him."

"How can you prevent him? Please, Gail, why don't you drop the whole idea? I can't bear to think of you being hurt."

"I'm hurt already, Rudi. It can't be any worse than it is now. But I don't intend to have Brett tagging along. I'll have to think of some way of stopping him."

Rudi was frowning. "Why does he want to go with you, Gail?"

"I wish I knew!"

"He was in love with you once. Perhaps he still feels the same way?"

I laughed shakily. "Oh no, it's not that! Brett doesn't care about me or Alexis or anyone else—except himself! He's just angry because that wretched film of his is ruined, and he thinks he's been made a fool of."

"Suppose . . . suppose I told him you had changed your mind about going? I know he's got to return to London this evening, and if he thinks you're not going to Majorca after all, you'll be able to slip away in the morning without Brett realizing."

"Oh, Rudi, would you really? I'd be so grateful."

He smiled ruefully. "You know I'd do anything for you, Gail. I'm dead set against the idea of you going at all, but if you must go, then I'd rather *he* wasn't with you."

Caterina, in her typically generous and thoughtful way, had sent Jenny through with a message that I wasn't to bother about preparing a meal as she would provide something for us. Promptly at seven-thirty her cook, Mary, appeared with a laden cart—a roast chicken and all the trimmings and a lemon mousse for dessert. But in spite of the excellent food, dinner was an uncomfortable meal for me.

Madeleine was there; she always came down to the dining room in the evening unless she was feeling particularly unwell. Freda Aiken sat with us too, making not the slightest effort to help while I served the meal. An agency nurse who knew her rights.

How different she was from Belle Forsyth! Belle, much more than a nurse-companion, had become virtually the housekeeper at Deer's Leap, always ready and willing to turn her hand to whatever needed doing. And she was a good cook, too.

I had liked Belle in every way. I found it almost as difficult to believe that she had ruthlessly deserted her patient as that Alexis had deserted his wife. And yet . . .

Tonight, the atmosphere around the table was edgy, none of us talking very much. It was as if we were all watching and waiting. There was one awkward moment when Madeleine turned to me, saying, "Gail, dear, you didn't tell me where it is you're going tomorrow."

"Oh, didn't I?" I hated having to lie to her. Poor Madeleine was so trusting that it was pathetically easy. "I've got to go up to London. It's an awful bore, but a rush job has cropped up."

She smiled at me sorrowfully. "It's really not fair, is it, darling? That firm of yours gives you a holiday, and then they expect you to go to the London office and work."

Across the table, Freda Aiken smirked at me, as if we were sharing some private joke. It made me feel tainted. Obviously, from her expression, she knew all about where I was going—and why. I wondered whether Rudi had told her, or if she'd picked it up as gossip from Jenny next door.

"I'll try not to be away for long, Madeleine," I said. "I'll be back just as soon as I can."

"And then you'll stay for a proper holiday, won't

you? I expect Alexis will be home when you get back, and we'll have a lovely time together."

That night I slept fitfully. After four months in New York I had forgotten the deep nocturnal silence of the countryside. Not an empty silence, but filled with tiny rustlings and stealthy movements. Every twig that brushed another could be heard, every drip of water, the faint far-off murmur of a passing car. I found myself breathing shallowly, trying to listen. But for what? I was glad when morning came at last.

I went down early to get myself some breakfast. While I was filling the kettle for coffee, the back door opened and Mrs. Cramp came walking in. She was a thin, shrewish woman in her forties, the latest of a string of domestic helps. Since Deer's Leap was rather isolated, it was difficult to get anyone to come the three and a half miles from the nearest village. Mrs. Cramp used a motor scooter, riding it in a curiously awkward, upright fashion.

"Oh, you're back then!" she said, taking off her coat to reveal a flowered apron tied tightly around her middle. "It's a funny business about your uncle, isn't it? He didn't seem the type to me, but you can never tell with men, can you? I wouldn't trust any man as far as I could throw him." She hung her coat on a hook behind the door and patted her mousy hair. "What's going to happen to Mrs. Karel, then?"

She would have settled down to a nice juicy chat, but I had no intention of discussing the situation with her.

"I'll be out of your way in a minute," I said, dropping a slice of bread into the toaster. "I've got a plane to catch, so I'm in rather a hurry."

Affronted, she went to the broom closet and started making a clatter. I shrugged and sat down to eat my breakfast hurriedly at the alcove table, scanning through the copy of the *Times* that I'd picked up in the hall. The news about Alexis was played down. But I wondered uneasily what the popular papers would be making of it.

There was something I had to do before saying
goodbye to Madeleine—something I found embarrass-
ingly difficult in the circumstances.

Caterina was an early riser, and, as expected, I
found her in their small breakfast room, alone. She was
wearing a purple silk housecoat trimmed with gold
and looked very splendid. Caterina, watching her figure, always kept to the light Continental breakfast, just
rolls and butter and fruit conserve, and there was a
delicious aroma of freshly made coffee. She greeted
me with a warm smile.

"Gail, my dear! Will you join me? Ralph won't be
down for at least another half hour."

She spoke artlessly, too kind to be making a deliberate point. But it was just further confirmation that Sir
Ralph's feelings about Alexis were reflected in his attitude to me. Caterina knew he wouldn't welcome my
company at the moment.

"Thank you," I said, "but I've just had my breakfast.
In any case I mustn't stop. I'll have to be off soon to
catch the plane."

She stopped pouring coffee to glance at me, puzzled.
"The plane?"

"Yes—to Palma."

"But, Gail, we understood from Brett that you had
given up the idea of going. Rudi told him. Ralph and I
were so relieved."

"Yes, well . . ." I said uneasily. "I've decided I will
go after all. That's why I've come to see you, actually.
Caterina, I hate having to impose on you when you've
been so wonderfully good already. I know how this
whole business has upset you and Sir Ralph. But, you
see, I shall worry dreadfully about Madeleine while
I'm away."

Putting down her coffee cup, Caterina stood up and
took my two hands in hers.

"My dear—*of course!* We cannot allow poor Madeleine to suffer any more than she must. I shall watch
over her with the greatest care, Gail. You need have
no fear of that."

"Oh thank you, Caterina! That makes me a lot hap-

pier in my mind. You don't know what a consolation it
it to me, to feel that you are right next door. I am not
much impressed by that new nurse."

"How are you getting to London Airport?" she
asked.

"By train. I'm going back now to ring for a taxi to
take me to the station."

"No, no, no!" She shook her head emphatically. "I'll
drive you."

"But I can't allow you to do that."

She looked at me reproachfully. "We are friends,
Gail, you and I, are we not? Please don't let this terrible trouble change our relationship. It's true that I
think you are unwise to go chasing after your uncle,
but if you have made up your mind, then please let
me do you this small service."

I capitulated in the face of her gentle persuasion.
"Thank you again. It would be a help not having to
bother with trains and worrying about connections."

Last night I had not unpacked properly but merely
transferred a few things I thought I might need into an
overnight case. I collected this from my bedroom and
went along to say goodbye to Madeleine. She was still
in bed. Freda Aiken had brought a tray of tea and
toast, and was busy plumping up Madeleine's pillows.
She was brisk, efficient and strong. No doubt an excellent nurse but without the saving grace of human
warmth.

"That will do, that will do!" Madeleine told her petu-
lantly. "Leave us now, please. I wish to talk to my
niece alone."

Freda Aiken withdrew, looking decidedly indignant,
and Madeleine said grudgingly, "She tries, I suppose,
but she is not like Belle." She sighed, and I thought I
saw tears glint in her pale golden eyes. "And now you
are off, Gail!"

"In a few minutes. I just looked in to say goodbye.
Caterina is driving me to ... to London."

"Is she? How nice for you both!"

Madeleine was in one of her difficult moods this
morning, and it made me feel doubly guilty about

leaving her. But I *knew* I was doing the right thing. I
need only be gone for a couple of days, and with any
luck Alexis would come back with me. With any
luck Madeleine need never discover what had happened. Surely if Alexis and I could talk for a few
minutes, I could make him understand the full implications of what he was doing. Make him realize the
harm not only to Madeleine but to everything he had
believed in and worked for all these years. I *must* be
able to make him see.

I bent and kissed my aunt on the cheek, but she remained unresponsive. I lingered a few moments longer,
trying to win her around, but in the end I had to leave
her without seeing any sign of a break in this bitter,
petulant mood.

Rudi was standing at the foot of the stairs.

"Gail, I wish you weren't going off like this. It's still
not too late to change your mind."

"Oh, Rudi, we had all that out yesterday."

He nodded helplessly. "It's just that I hate to think
of you being hurt. At least promise one thing—that
you'll keep in touch. Will you phone me tonight and
let me know what's happening?"

I felt moved by his concern for me. Tears pricked
my eyelids and I had to blink them away. For a long
time I had known that Rudi was in love with me. I was
terribly fond of him, and if it hadn't been for Brett,
then perhaps . . .

"Yes, of course I'll phone you, Rudi. I must go now.
Here's Caterina."

Through the long hall window I could see the car
coming across from the stable-block, a bright-red Fiat.
Caterina had become quite Anglicized since marrying
Sir Ralph, but she still had her Continental breakfast
each morning and chose an Italian car for herself. And
her warm, impulsive, Latin nature—nothing would
ever alter that.

As we drove off, Rudi stood waving from the doorway. Glancing up at the house, I saw a quick movement, someone backing swiftly out of sight. Freda
Aiken or Mrs. Cramp, indulging their morbid curiosity.

I sighed unhappily. It wasn't any longer the Deer's Leap I had known and loved these past years.

Chapter Five

Caterina's volatile nature never allowed her to remain silent for long. She chatted as she drove, commenting on the traffic, the places we passed through, reminiscing whenever something triggered off a memory. But presently she became serious.

"Gail, there is something I want to say, something it is important for you to understand. In spite of all this unpleasantness, Ralph still has the greatest feeling of sympathy for Madeleine. There will always be a home for her at Deer's Leap. And for you, of course."

Already, I noted sadly, Alexis was written off completely. But I was going to reinstate him in the minds of Sir Ralph and Caterina—and of everyone else, too. How, I didn't yet know. I had only my own determination to guide me.

I mumbled my thanks to Caterina, which she brushed aside. Then she shot me a shrewd, appraising glance.

"Brett is very concerned, Gail."

"Yes, I know." I was unable to conceal the bitterness I felt. "That film of his is just so much useless junk now, he says. And of course he's angry because his father has been so upset."

"Oh, but I didn't quite mean that, Gail. Brett is concerned about *you*."

"Concerned about *me!*" I tried to pass if off with a light laugh. "That'll be the day!"

"It was, once," she said, and her voice sounded sad. "Neither of you told us very much, but we knew you were seeing a good deal of each other in London. For a time Ralph and I thought——"

"Then you got it wrong!" I said brusquely. "Look, Caterina, wouldn't it be better to go through Staines?

There should be less traffic on that road."

A change of route, a change of conversation. After that, Caterina began asking how I liked America. In her singing days before she met and married Sir Ralph, she had traveled all over the world. She had sung Verdi and Puccini in Chicago and at the Met in New York, and had given concerts in many other American cities.

We reached the airport in good time. Emerging from the approach tunnel, we parked the car and went to collect the ticket I'd booked by phone. The desk was very busy, and we had to stand around waiting.

Caterina asked if I was sure I had everything I needed. Did I have sufficient money? She could easily lend me some.

"Thanks, but I'll be okay. I brought back my bank balance from the States in traveler's checks. It'll be enough to cover this trip."

I was still talking when I felt it, a sharp strong tug at my handbag. My fingers tightened, too late. The bag was gone.

I gasped and spun round, my eyes searching wildly in all directions. But there were so many people milling about that I couldn't pick out the thief.

"Gail, whatever is the matter?" asked Caterina, beside me.

"My bag! Someone snatched my handbag! Did you see who it was?" With a sickening rush, the full extent of my loss hit me. "Oh, Caterina, what am I going to do? It's got my passport and money and everything."

The girl at the desk was quick off the mark. The phone was already in her hand. "I'm calling the airport police. Can you give me a description of the man?"

"I didn't even see him," I said miserably. "He snatched it from behind. It's a black patent bag, with a strap."

I felt a terrible wave of frustration, of helplessness, of sheer panic.

Hearing a sudden commotion somewhere across the lobby, I turned to look. Other people were staring, too, but in the confusion I couldn't make out what was happening. Then, like a miracle, I saw a tall man pushing his way toward me, waving my handbag above his head.

"This is yours, miss, I think," he said, presenting it to me.

"Oh, thank you! That's marvelous! I was feeling desperate, wondering what on earth I was going to do."

"You'd better make sure nothing is missing," he suggested.

The clasp was still fastened. I unclipped it and took a quick look inside. Passport, wallet—both safe. A tidal wave of relief flooded through me. "I . . . I really don't know how to thank you enough." I stammered. "What happened, exactly?"

"Well, I was standing over there waiting around for my wife, and I happened to notice this little guy snatch your purse. He made off fast, dodging into the crowd, and I lost sight of him. But a couple of seconds later he came right past me, and I grabbed at him. Unfortunately, I couldn't hold him—these sneak thieves are as slippery as eels—and it was all so quick I don't think other people realized what was going on. I'm afraid he got clean away. Still, he dropped your purse, that's the main thing."

"I'm so very grateful to you!"

"Glad to have been of service." He smiled, gave me an embarrassed little bow, and strode away.

It needed several minutes for my heartbeat to slow back to normal. I'd had a very narrow escape. Without my handbag, it wouldn't have been possible to go on to Majorca. A phone call to my bank might have replaced the stolen money, but it would probably have taken days and days to replace a lost passport.

There was half an hour before the plane was due to leave. Caterina wanted to wait with me, but I wouldn't let her. I knew that Sir Ralph disapproved of my going to Majorca. I didn't want to keep Caterina away from home for too long and give him something else to hold against me.

Tears glistened in her eyes as she kissed me good-bye. "I still wish you wouldn't go! Take care of yourself, my dear one."

"I'll be okay. Don't worry! You've been so sweet and kind, Caterina. One day I'll be able to thank you properly."

The time seemed to crawl by when she had gone. But at last the formalities were over, and I waited with a group of other passengers to board the plane.

From close behind me a low voice murmured into my ear, "That wasn't very clever of you, Gail."

Brett! I spun around and stared at him.

"What are you doing here?" I asked faintly.

He held up a canvas airline bag for me to see.

"I told you that if you were mad enough to go to Majorca, then I was coming with you. But I didn't expect you'd try and pull a fast one like that. I barely had time to make a reservation."

I seethed with fury. "How did you find out? Was it Caterina who told you?"

"Does it matter how I found out? Actually, it was that Mrs. Cramp. I called you at Deer's Leap this morning to ask how things were going, and she told me you'd gone off in a hurry to catch a plane."

"She'd no right to!" I said in bitter dismay.

Brett and I didn't speak again until we had boarded the plane. Without asking, he dropped into the seat next to me.

"Why are you doing this, Brett?" I demanded.

"More to the point, why are *you* doing it? What do you hope to gain?"

He wouldn't understand. He didn't want to understand. I said in an angry undertone, "I'm not obliged to explain my actions to you, Brett."

"Maybe not. But you'd be well advised to try and explain them to yourself. Get this into your skull, Gail— your uncle could hardly have made it plainer that he doesn't care a damn what you or anyone else thinks of him. He's opted out, and to hell with all those lofty ideals he was supposed to stand for. Okay, so he's got his hands on more money than he's ever had in his life before . . . and a beautiful woman to help him spend it. He's not the first man to lose his head like that, and he won't be the last. But I wish to God he'd picked a less crucial time. Why did he have to wait until the film was nine-tenths made?"

"That's all you care about, isn't it?" I muttered savagely.

"If you really think so, Gail. . . . But I think you're wrong."

The gray winter day stretched on interminably as we flew across France. I refused to discuss Alexis any further, and there was little else for Brett and I to talk about. Or too many things! For most of the time we were locked in a tight silence, except for an occasional frozen courtesy. I could never for a single instant forget that it was Brett who sat next to me; and sometimes, accidentally, we touched. My brain spun with memories of the time we had spent together. The pain of it was almost more than I could bear.

Then we were over the Mediterranean, nearing the end of our journey, and the sun broke through at last. Quite suddenly the air was clear, only the far horizon veiled with a soft lilac haze. Far below, a ship scored a line of gold across the glittering cobalt sea.

Out of the misty distance an island emerged, rugged mountains and deep valleys, wild and beautiful. As we crossed the coastal range and dipped lower, there appeared to be a white gauze laid upon the land. "That's the almond trees in bloom," said a man in the seat behind us, and a sigh of delight rippled among the passengers. So much beauty, yet today it only made me sad.

Once we landed, I wasted no breath trying to argue with Brett. I let him find us a taxi, and immediately he gave the driver the name of the hotel where Alexis was reported to be staying.

The taxi rattled along noisily in a stream of fast-moving traffic, flashing past orchards of almond trees and the quaint Majorcan windmills that whirled around like children's toys. It took only a few minutes to

reach Palma, where the buildings struck me as Italian-
ate rather than Spanish. Down by the harbor we joined
a broad modern highway that curved around the arc
of the bay. It was absurdly warm for February.

"This is the place for a winter holiday," Brett remarked. "Who wants to be in England at this time of
year?"

A winter holiday . . . with Brett! Twelve months
ago that would have been one of my dreams. Now, for
all the warmth of the sun, I felt frozen inside.

With the moment of truth, my confrontation with
Alexis, so near, I had to think how I could shake Brett
off. I was determined to see my uncle alone. Without
Brett, if possible without Belle Forsyth.

We swept on around the bay, where white-sailed
boats gracefully skimmed the water. Here the hotels
became more widely spaced—shining new towers,
each with tier upon tier of balconies overlooking the
sea; swimming pools and terrace restaurants. A holiday
paradise.

The taxi swerved into an entrance, climbed a steep
curving driveway, and pulled up by wide chrome-and-
glass doors flung open to the warm afternoon.

"Alexis is certainly doing things in style," Brett
commented dryly.

We entered and went to inquire at the desk. The
clerk, a handsome olive-skinned young Spaniard, informed us aloofly that Dr. Karel was not in the hotel at
the moment.

How stupid of me to have imagined Alexis would
be sitting around here, as if waiting for me to turn up!
But I had got myself to such a peak of tension that I
felt a terrible sense of letdown.

"Do you know where he is?" Brett asked. "Or when
he'll be back?"

"I regret, *señor*, I do not."

Brett looked at me. "I suppose we'd better check
ourselves in, then. We'll have to stay the night somewhere, and we might as well be on the spot."

"Yes, all right."

Once he knew we were to be guests ourselves, the

clerk unbent a little. While consulting the register he volunteered the information that Dr. Karel and Miss Forsyth were not expected to be dining in the hotel that evening.

Yet I had a feeling that he wasn't telling us everything he knew; his manner was a shade too smooth. Brett seemed to notice nothing, and I kept my suspicions to myself. If I was going to pump the clerk for information, I'd prefer to do it alone.

We were given two rooms on opposite sides of the corridor, on the fifth floor. As we parted outside my door, Brett said, "I'll come and collect you in fifteen minutes? Let's have a drink and decide what we're going to do. Okay?"

"Make it half an hour, will you? I must have a shower."

"Not a bad idea. I think I will, too."

Once in my room, I flung myself into action, showering and dressing in ten minutes flat. Then, stealthily, I opened my door and peered into the corridor. Everything was quiet. Brett's door was safely closed. I sped along to the stairs and went down a floor before summoning the elevator, just in case Brett should come out of his room and see me waiting.

As I'd been hoping, now that I was alone the desk clerk's attitude was subtly different. He gave me his full attention.

"Yes, *señora* . . . ?"

"Just between the two of us," I wheedled, "are you quite sure you don't know where Dr. Karel is?"

He shook his head, smiling at me regretfully. "You are from an English newspaper? There have been so many reporters, and Dr. Karel is not pleased with the way they have pestered him."

"I'm not a reporter, oh no!"

He looked at me hesitantly, and I became more than ever convinced that he was concealing something.

"Please," I begged. "I must see him. I'm a relative. It's terribly urgent."

In the end he gave way gracefully. "I can only tell you this, *señora*. Dr. Karel asked me if I could recom-

mend a restaurant in Palma, and I told him the Velasquez was an excellent place. It is possible that he and
Miss Forsyth will dine there this evening, though of
course I cannot promise."

The time for dinner was still hours away. But this
might be the only chance I'd get of escaping from Brett.

"Haven't you any idea at all where they might be
now?"

He shrugged. I was being too persistent. "Sightsee-
ing, perhaps. There is much to interest visitors on the
island."

The only thing, I decided, was to kill time on my
own until there was hope of finding Alexis at the restaurant. I asked the clerk to cash a traveler's check
for me and ordered a taxi.

"One more thing," I said as I was leaving. "The
gentleman I came with . . . please say nothing to him
about where I'm going."

He nodded, smiling at me like a conspirator.

I asked the taxi driver to drop me off somewhere in
the center of Palma. I found I was in a wide, busy
street called (of course) the Avenida Generalissimo
Franco. I began to stroll aimlessly.

For a while I kept to the main thoroughfares, glancing at the shops with their rich displays of old lace and
mantillas, Moorish jewelery, and exquisite embroidery,
all the time keeping a faintly hopeful lookout for
Alexis and Belle. Then suddenly it struck me that by
now Brett must have realized I had given him the slip.
He might come searching for me.

The huge mass of the Gothic cathedral rose ahead
of me, and I decided to take refuge in there.

Entering, I was pounced on eagerly by guides. But I
was there to get through unwanted time, not to sight-
see. I evaded them and wandered alone in the cool,
echoing nave. Even in my present withdrawn mood, I
could not help being affected by the atmosphere—the
magnificence of the lofty vaulted roof, the brilliant
bold colors of the stained glass. After a time I sat down
quietly at the back of the little side chapel and listened
while Mass was celebrated.

When I came outside again I found that darkness had fallen swiftly. The air was cooler now, and I was glad I had brought my coat. I strolled down by the harbor. Lights from all around the bay sent shimmering bars of gold across the water.

I became aware that I was being followed, which wasn't really surprising. I decided I had better not stay on the streets. Flamenco music poured from a café a few yards along, so I went inside and ordered a glass of sherry.

Here, too, I was looked at or over. Two or three times a man passed by my table and tried to pick me up. Politeness failing, I found a hard frozen stare was the answer.

My glass was nearly empty, but I didn't want another drink. So I sat for long minutes with the dregs of my sherry until at last I judged that the time had come to move on to the restaurant.

It turned out to be quite close, but the moment I stepped inside I realized I was still much too early. The place was almost empty. I chose a table in an alcove from which I could see the entrance and resigned myself to a long wait.

The Velasquez restaurant gave an impression of slightly faded magnificence—tall fluted columns and elegant potted palms, red velvet drapes and a carpet of royal blue and gold. The food was superb—if only I had been in a mood to enjoy it. I accepted the waiter's inevitable recommendation of a paella and ate it without interest, watching the door with every forkful.

I lingered over dessert, a rich chocolate gâteau, and took almost an hour over coffee. In the end I had to admit defeat. There had been no guarantee that Alexis and Belle would come here, but even so I was left with a cold feeling of desolation.

Wearily, I signaled the waiter and asked for my bill. The amount of it shook me. If this was anything to go by, how much was staying at the hotel going to cost? I couldn't stay there at this rate for long.

With economy in mind, I asked the doorman if I could catch a bus back to my hotel, which was in the

Torreño quarter. He looked down his nose at me—
customers of the Velasquez weren't expected to travel
by bus! But he gave me directions, speaking English
with such a thick, lisping accent that I found it difficult
to follow.

I started walking, my steps heavy with disappointment. I wondered what I was going to say to Brett; he
would be furious with me for running out on him. I
had counted on finding Alexis. I had not allowed for
failure.

The street I had turned into on my way to the bus
was a narrow one, cobbled, with tall shuttered buildings on either side. Though I could see bright lights and
traffic passing right at the far end, the street itself was
dark and utterly deserted. I couldn't help a tremor of
unease.

As I stood hesitating on the narrow pavement, de-
bating whether this could really be the right way, a
car swung slowly around the corner from behind me. I
turned. Its headlights, full on, were so bright that I
was blinded. I stepped back instinctively, closer to the
wall.

The car came on, accelerating hard. It seemed to be
heading straight for me, even though I must have been
clearly visible. It had actually mounted the pavement
and still was coming on! Oh, God, it couldn't possibly
stop in time! Panic-stricken, I screamed and pressed
myself back against a door in the wall. But nothing
could save me now.

Then, in that final, ultimate split second, the door
behind me sprung open, and I fell sprawling backward.

The car went by with a roar, almost scraping the
bricks of the wall, and suddenly it was darkness again.
Pitchblack. I lay where I had fallen, shaking uncon-
trollably. For the moment I was too terrified to think
of anything beyond the one stark fact that I had escaped certain death only by a hairsbreadth.

Chapter Six

Somewhere close at hand behind me I heard another door opening, and light streamed out. A startled voice gasped something I didn't understand. Lifting my head, I saw a stout woman dressed all in black. She stared down at me with wide, astonished eyes, then came forward and helped me to my feet, talking rapidly and incomprehensibly.

"English . . ." I mumbled apologetically. *"Inglesa."* Then I tried French. *"Je suis Anglaise."*

She seemed to understand and nodded and smiled reassuringly, while still pouring a flood of words meaningless to me. Gripping my arm, she urged me toward the lighted doorway. Only now did I begin to take in any details. I was in a narrow dark alleyway with rough stone walls, and I realized that it must be an outside passageway between two buildings.

As we went inside, the smell of garlic was almost overpowering. It seemed to saturate the air so that I felt sickened, and I was reluctant to penetrate any further. But my legs were so weak that I needed to sit down, and I could hardly do that in the street. Besides, I was scared to leave this refuge. Though I felt a little lightheaded from shock, I knew with chilling clarity that the car had been driven at me deliberately! The driver, whoever he was, had intended to kill me. But why?

The single light in the room came from a central unshaded bulb and showed me this was a poor home. The furniture was worn, the walls were a grimy beige color. There was an old man who sat in a wooden armchair drawn up to the table. He seemed to be affected by some sort of nervous ague, for his thin blue-veined hands trembled. Beside him stood a small girl with long pigtails and a black-haired, dark-skinned boy of fifteen or sixteen. Their eyes were all turned upon me, staring.

The woman pushed me down onto the shabby sofa and immediately went to a corner cupboard and fetched a bottle and glass. Gratefully, I gulped down the amber liquid and found it raw and strong, stinging my throat. But it seemed to revive me.

The youth stepped forward, speaking diffidently. "You are English, *señora?*"

"Yes, yes, that's right." I felt so relieved that someone could understand me that I babbled on. "There was a car . . . it drove straight at me. If your street door hadn't been unlatched, I would certainly have been killed."

He was gazing at me blankly, and I realized I had gone too fast for him to follow me. I began again.

"A motorcar, you understand? An automobile."

He nodded, his thin strong-boned face lighting up eagerly. *"Si, si . . .* an *automovil."*

"The driver . . . he tried to knock me down . . . tried to kill me."

He looked bewildered and said something to his mother. She answered in another torrent of words. Then the old man, who was presumably the grandfather, joined in, and the little girl spoke in a high piping voice. They were all staring at me, almost as if I was some creature from another planet. At length the boy began fumbling for more English words.

"Steal . . . ? He take money?"

"No, not steal." I held up my handbag, which I had been clutching all this time without knowing it. "He didn't stop. He just tried to run me down. Kill me."

Their scared, uncomprehending eyes looked back at me. What was the use? The alcohol was already having an effect, and I could feel the shivering of my limbs growing less. I sought about in my mind for something they would understand, some explanation that would satisfy them.

"Accident," I said. *"Comprende?* Accident."

They all repeated the word solemnly, even the little

girl, though whether it meant anything to them I couldn't be sure. I reached forward to put the glass on the table; then, experimentally, I tried to stand up. My legs still felt weak, but I decided I would just about be able to manage. I nodded to each one of them in turn—the old man, the boy, the little girl, and lastly to the woman.

"*Gracias,*" I said, moving toward the door. "*Mucho gracias.*"

"You go now?" asked the boy.

"Yes," I said. "*Si si* . . . I must go."

"You walk?" he said. "*La señora . . . sola!* It is dark!"

"I was going to get a bus," I told him. But that meant nothing to him. I tried again. "Taxi."

"Ah, *taxi!*"

There was another family discussion, concluding in nods all around. Then the boy announced, with a sort of gallant pride, "I, Pedro, will come with you."

I smiled my gratitude. The thought of emerging into the dark streets again terrified me. Maybe the unknown driver who wanted me dead was still lurking there, waiting for a second chance to run me down. I knew that it would take all my courage to leave the safety of this room, even with the friendly boy escorting me.

Outside, I wondered why I had ever been so foolhardy as to take this turning at all. Although linking two busy traffic routes, the narrow street was in almost total darkness, shadowed by the tall, high-walled buildings. As I walked beside Pedro to the farther end, I was shaking with nerves. My eyes kept searching for doorways where we might take shelter if the car should return. But mercifully, the street remained empty.

We reached the corner at last and were among other people again. At once I felt safer and let out my breath in a long sigh of relief.

Pedro did not slacken his pace, and I presumed he knew where he could find me a taxi. All I wanted now was to sink back in a soft-padded seat and be whisked straight to the hotel. Encountering Brett no longer seemed a problem. His face would look comfortingly friendly, even though he might be in a bad mood because I'd walked out on him.

"Gail! Gail!"

I heard my name shouted from across the street, above the din of the traffic. In bewilderment, I stopped and gazed around, wondering if I had only imagined Brett's voice because he'd been in my mind. Then I saw him on the pavement opposite, waving at me frantically. He started to cross, dodging nimbly between the fast-moving cars.

"Where the hell have you been?" he asked in a belligerent tone as he reached me. "And who's this?"

Pedro looked startled, and to reassure him I said quickly, "It's all right. Friend . . . *amigo.*"

Brett said impatiently, "Will you please explain what's going on, Gail? I've been searching for you all over the place, and then I find you calmly wandering the streets with a local youth."

He was angry, all right! But he was still Brett. I would be safe now as long as I stayed with him. In my pent-up state I clutched his arm.

"Somebody tried to kill me, Brett! Quite deliberately. A car just tried to run me down."

He looked at me with cool incredulity. "Gail, you're imagining things! The way some of them drive here is pretty irresponsible, I agree, but whoever would deliberately want to run you down?"

"I don't know who it was," I shouted. "But I was walking through a narrow street back there . . . on my way to catch a bus, when a car came along from behind. Suddenly it accelerated and drove straight at me. If I hadn't fallen backward into a doorway, I'd have been *killed!*"

My voice had risen to the edge of hysteria. Brett held me against him and patted me soothingly, as if I was a child to be comforted.

"It's all right, love—it's all right. I'll get you back to the hotel. But you still haven't told me who this young chap is."

It was difficult to explain it all, confronted by Brett's

evident disbelief. Pedro stood looking on, nodding his head vigorously, though he couldn't have made much sense of my incoherent story.

"You do seem to have had a narrow escape," said Brett when I stammered to an end. "But you must forget this crazy idea about someone trying to kill you, Gail. Obviously, it was just some drunk." His hand went to his pocket. "I suppose I'd better pay off your escort."

Pedro understood the gesture, if not the words. He backed away, his manhood insulted.

"No, not to pay money! I do not wish." He turned to me, still concerned on my behalf. "You okay now, yes?"

I nodded, pulling myself together and smiling at him.

"Yes, I am okay now. Thank you for being so very kind and helpful, Pedro. And please thank your mother again, too."

Brett surprised me by adding a few words in Spanish. With an oddly appealing little bow, the boy turned and walked off quickly.

"Come on," said Brett. "Let's find a taxi and get back to the hotel."

"But shouldn't we report this to the police? Someone tried to kill me!"

"For God's sake!" snapped Brett irritably. "You've said yourself there was nobody around when it happened, nobody who could back up your word. Just suppose we could get the police to believe your story that it was no accident, but done quite deliberately— what then? What could you tell them to help them track down the culprit? You couldn't describe the car, could you? Or the driver?" He shot me a keen, probing look. "Well, could you?"

I shook my head unhappily. "All the same . . ."

Brett cut across me. "The sum total of going to the police would be to start a lot of inquiries we don't want. So far, Gail, we've been lucky. So far the press haven't got on to the fact that you're Alexis Karel's niece who's come to try and persuade him to return home. But if they do, and you stir up trouble with the police, just

think of the headlines—'Runaway's niece claims someone tried to kill her.' "

"All right, you've made your point. So we've just got
to let him get away with it?"

Brett pounced on the word. "Him?"

"I mean, whoever was driving the car."

"Forget it, Gail. Put the incident right out of your
mind. If there really *was* anything deliberate involved,
and it wasn't just a drunk driver who couldn't control
his car, then my guess is that it must have been some
young hooligan who thought it would be fun to give you
a scare."

"A scare! But I'd have been killed, I tell you, if that
door hadn't given way."

He nodded, frowning. "I realize you've had a nasty
shock, but you mustn't get it out of proportion. Honestly, I should try and forget the whole thing, or you'll
finish up with a persecution complex."

It was easy for Brett to say forget it. But how could
I ever forget that car roaring toward me with its headlights blazing, blinding me, almost touching the wall
where I cowered helplessly?

Brett found us a taxi, and I climbed in almost in a
trance. I was so deeply absorbed that when Brett spoke
his words hardly registered at first.

"If you hadn't gone off like that, Gail, I could have
told you there isn't a chance of finding Alexis in Palma.
He's skipped out. He's left Majorca."

"Left Majorca!" I surfaced with a jolt. "Where is he,
then?"

It was dark in the taxi. Lights from outside gave me
flashed glimpses of Brett's face. I couldn't read his expression, but he sounded pleased with himself, almost
smug.

"At the present moment your dear uncle and his girl
friend are somewhere at sea aboard a fishing boat,
heading for some destination unknown. They left this
afternoon before we even arrived."

"But I don't understand. Why weren't we told at the
hotel that they'd checked out? The desk clerk said—"

"The desk clerk was no doubt well bribed by Alexis to put inquirers off the scent. Your uncle didn't want anyone to know they'd left the island."

"But why not? What's it all about, Brett? How did you come to find out, anyway?"

"I happened to run into a chap I know in the hotel lobby. Dougal Fraser. He works for the *Globe,* and he shot over here yesterday when the story first broke about Alexis and Belle turning up in Majorca. Dougal actually had an interview with your uncle. He says Alexis kept complaining about being hounded by the press, saying he's a private citizen, a naturalized British subject, and that what he does is entirely his own concern and no one else's. And now, apparently, he's fixed a deal with a fisherman to take them off the island secretly. Not a soul knows where they're heading."

I felt stricken, engulfed by an agonizing sense of failure. That this blow should come scarcely half an hour after I'd narrowly escaped death in a dark side street! I closed my eyes, fighting tears that threatened to sweep away the last shreds of my self-control.

"Where . . . where do you think they can have gone?" I faltered.

Brett hunched his shoulders. "The possibilities are endless, right around the compass. Algeria, the east coast of Spain, the French Riviera, Corsica, Sardinia. Or maybe just one of the other Balearic Islands—Minorca or Ibiza. It looks as if Alexis has achieved the exact reverse of what he hoped for. He won't be left in peace now. As Dougal pointed out, if they had just hung around here in Majorca the story would have died a natural death in a couple of days. But now the press is on the alert again. This has given the whole thing a new lease on life."

"So what do we do now?" I asked miserably.

"We pack up and go home, if we're sensible."

"No, Brett, I can't. Not without trying to find him."

"Then we just stay put until we get some news."

"You mean, just wait here?"

"Have you any better idea?" He slung the words at

me. But when I didn't answer, he added more gently, "I don't think it will be for long, Gail. It seems certain they weren't equipped for a lengthy voyage. They'll have to make some landfall in the next twenty-four hours or so, and the minute word comes through we can get after them."

"Plus every reporter within range, I suppose," I said bitterly. "Why can't Alexis see that he's playing into the hands of the gutter press? At this rate we'll never be able to keep it from Madeleine."

Brett said curtly, "Just you remember, Gail, that if it wasn't for the newspapers you'd never have got onto Alexis as fast as this—if at all. And as for your aunt, that's your own lookout. It was a stupid idea to try and keep her in the dark."

I bit my lip. I should have known better than to expect sympathy from Brett. And yet I had to acknowledge that I needed him at this moment. I needed his contacts in the newspaper world if I was to get after Alexis in time to save the situation. Every day, every hour that passed, the chance of Madeleine finding out grew more likely. Rudi couldn't keep her in the dark indefinitely. If she happened to ask for a newspaper, he could hardly refuse to give her one. And Madeleine had a radio in her room, though she almost never switched it on.

I remembered how desperate I had been to come to Majorca without Brett. Now I was glad that he had found me out. But I would have to watch my step with him. I couldn't afford to go on risking his anger. I didn't want him to rush off in a fit of temper.

In an effort to placate him, I said, "Perhaps I made a mistake deciding not to tell Madeleine, only at the time it seemed best. A shock like that . . . I didn't know how she'd react. I just felt I had to try and talk to Alexis, to try and persuade him to come home before it was too late. And now I've got this far, Brett, I can't give up. Not yet."

In the darkness of the taxi, I felt his fingers touch my wrist, resting there for an instant. Considering that he and I had once been lovers, it was a trivial gesture. But the effect upon me was out of all proportion. I felt suddenly breathless and had to fight a wild yearning to throw myself into his arms.

Chapter Seven

There was a disturbing feeling of intimacy about staying the night under the same roof as Brett, in a bedroom just across the corridor from him. I wondered if he was conscious of it, too. I wondered if it brought back to him, as vividly as it did to me, the other times we had been together.

Not that this palatial hotel was anything like the places we had stayed at before. We had chosen sleepy country pubs where we felt shut away from the outside world, where they served roast beef and Yorkshire pudding for dinner and a huge platter of bacon and eggs to entice us down in the morning. We'd had a special favorite, an ancient millhouse lying in a fold of the Sussex Downs, a few miles inland from Brighton. Our bedroom was cozy under the thatch, with heavy oaken beams and beeswax-scented furniture. The whispering of water from the stream outside was a gentle background to the night hours.

A favorite place! My memory was running riot; in reality Brett and I had stayed there only twice.

The white telephone on the bedside table reminded me that I had promised to call Rudi. I felt a curious reluctance, but I wanted to ask about Madeleine, too. The operator told me there would be a delay, so I undressed and slipped into bed. I waited with growing impatience for over an hour before at last the call came through.

"Rudi, it's Gail. Is everything all right? How is Madeleine?"

"She still suspects nothing, thank heaven!" he told

me. "But, Gail, you're so late phoning me. I've been worried, expecting a call the whole evening. Have you seen Alexis? What did he say?"

"No, I haven't been able to contact him, not yet."

"Why not? Is something wrong, Gail?"

"The thing is, Alexis and Belle left Majorca before we even got here."

"*Left?*"

"They hired a fishing boat, and we don't know where they're heading for."

"I see!" There was a brief pause. "Gail, you said 'we.' Who do you mean?"

Why did I hesitate? Rudi would have to know sooner or later.

"Brett is here too," I said slowly. "He turned up at London Airport just before the plane took off."

"But how did he know you were going? I told him you'd decided not to."

"It seems he phoned Deer's Leap this morning, and Mrs. Cramp told him I'd gone to catch a plane. So he put two and two together."

"Damn the woman! You can't stop her from gossiping."

I said quickly, "There's no real harm done. Brett isn't being a nuisance or anything." I didn't add that I was actually glad, now, to have Brett here with me.

"What are you going to do, Gail? I suppose you'll come straight back home, won't you?"

"No, I'm staying here until we get news of where they've gone. It shouldn't be long—not more than a few hours, according to Brett."

Rudi asked, with a sudden rush of suspicion, "Is Brett there with you now?"

"No, we separated over an hour ago. I'm in bed now. We've checked in at the same hotel where Alexis was staying."

There was silence at the other end of the line. I wanted to end this pointless conversation, yet I couldn't bring myself to hang up on Rudi.

"I can't help feeling anxious about you, Gail," he

said at last. "Being there with Brett. I know how deeply he hurt you once before. I don't want that to happen again. I beg you, please come home."

"I can't, Rudi! And you don't need to worry about me—at least not because of Brett. It was all over between us long ago. Finished and dead. It could never happen again."

"Then why is he in Majorca with you?"

It was a question I'd been asking myself constantly, a question I could find no answer to. I fell back on repetition. "I tell you it's all over between us. Surely you could see that for yourself, when Brett and I met at Deer's Leap yesterday."

"Perhaps," said Rudi. He made one last attempt. "Gail, if you have no more news of Alexis within the next twenty-four hours, then will you agree to give up and come home to England?"

"I can't promise anything, Rudi. But I'll call you again sometime tomorrow. Tell Madeleine I phoned, will you, and give her my love. And Caterina. Goodbye for now."

For a moment my hand lingered on the telephone, reluctant to give up the feeling of closeness with Deer's Leap. Then I turned off the bedside lamp and lay back. I felt tired to the point of exhaustion, yet I knew it would be hard to sleep.

My mind was dazed, bewildered by the day's swift flow of events. More than once when sleep was edging up on me, a knife-thrust memory of glaring yellow headlights and the scream of a revving engine brought me snapping back to wakefulness. I was left weak and shaking from the sudden recall of those terrifying seconds when my death had seemed a certainty.

But I must have slept, because I wakened to a new day.

Brett and I breakfasted on the paved terrace that overlooked the bay. A soft breeze blew in off the sea, and the golden sun shone down on us. It was blissfully warm—February like April sometimes is in England.

Below us, a sloping shrub garden hid the traffic-busy Paseo Maritimo that rimmed the sea. Mimosa and almond trees nodded their delicate blossoms, and freesias grew at their feet. The air was filled with birdsong.

On such a glorious morning I couldn't believe that things were really as bad as they had seemed last night. I felt bright with confidence that today we would get news of Alexis, news that would lead us to him. And when I had seen him, talked to him, then everything would come right again. As if the clock had miraculously been turned back.

I was going to succeed. I *had* to succeed. To fail would play right into the hands of Alexis's enemies. My uncle, I felt convinced, could have no idea how his present behavior was aiding the Communist cause— deserting the wife who had suffered so deeply on his behalf; seeming to turn his back on millions of friends and admirers; callously abandoning the refugees he had always helped—and now leading a life of ostentatious luxury! As a piece of propaganda for the Communists, it was devastating.

Nobody who was not on their side, openly or secretly, could wish me to fail in my mission.

Brett signaled the waiter. "Could you get me an English newspaper, do you think?"

"*Si, señor.* I will send for one."

The paper, when it came, was yesterday's edition, which Brett had already seen in London. He handed it to me. "You'd better read it and see what they're saying about Alexis. He's certainly been given the treatment."

The story began on page one and continued on an inside page. There were pictures of them both—Alexis walking on the grounds at Deer's Leap, the lake in the background. I recognized it as the one chosen for the dust jacket of his book. It was a splendid likeness of him, showing the strong jawline and fine intelligent eyes, the thick white hair which made him look so distinguished.

But the photograph of Belle was quite something else. Where the paper had dug it up I couldn't imagine. Very overposed, it made Belle look cheap and tarty, completely lacking the cool, poised beauty that characterized her. Maybe it was because her hair was shaken loose about her shoulders instead of in the neat coil she usually wore.

Miserably, I passed the newspaper back to Brett. "They make it all sound so horribly sordid."

"How would you describe it, then? Romantic?"

I had taken all I could stand of Brett's cynicism about Alexis. But as I started to denounce him for it, he laid a warning hand on my arm.

"Look out! Here comes Dougal Fraser."

I saw a man's head and shoulders moving among the shrubs of the sloping garden and realized there must be a zigzag path leading up from the promenade to the hotel terrace. Brett hailed him, and the man waved back.

Leaning toward me, Brett said, "Don't show too much interest in Alexis. Dougal doesn't realize who you are, and it's better to keep him ignorant."

"Who does he think I am, then?"

Brett gave me an odd look. "Gail, you've got to understand that if it leaked out to the press boys that you're Alexis Karel's niece, they'd be after you like a pack of wolves. It would put new meat on the bones of a tired story—the way you've come flying out here to bring your errant uncle to heel."

"Why do you always have to put things . . . ?" I began. But again he touched my arm.

"Careful! He'll be here in a second. Wipe that angry expression off your face and smile sweetly. Come on now—as far as Dougal Fraser or anyone else in Majorca is concerned, you're my girl friend."

I stared at him, frowning. "Is that what you've been saying?"

Brett's eyes narrowed swiftly. "Is it such a difficult thing to pretend, Gail?"

Perhaps it was as well I had no time to answer that. Dougal Fraser sprang up the last of the steps and came striding over to our table. He was around thirty years old, big-boned and tall—taller even than Brett—with sandy hair and very deep-blue eyes. Outwardly, he had a cheerful, carefree manner. Inwardly, I guessed, he would be very shrewd. When he spoke his voice had the attractive lilt of the Highlands.

"Hi, Brett! You seem to be enjoying life, lazing around in the sun, taking it easy."

Brett leaned back and hooked an extra chair for him from the next table. Dougal flopped into it and proceeded to look me over. "Some people," he remarked to Brett, "have all the luck!"

Brett signaled the waiter to bring another cup for Dougal. "I thought you were going to phone me. Why come yourself—is there some news?"

"Yes. But I don't trust the telephone when there are too many press guys around. So I thought I'd stroll over and see you."

I couldn't contain myself a second longer. "What *is* the news? Where is Alexis—er, Dr. Karel, I mean?"

Dougal turned his blue eyes on me, speculatively. Brett gave an uneasy laugh. "Gail's even more burned up than I am about my film being ruined."

"So it seems!" Dougal shrugged. "The fishing boat they're on is still at sea. But I've got a few contacts with airline people, and I've just had a call from the captain of a freight plane which landed at Marseilles this morning that he spotted *La Golondrina* soon after sunup. A positive identification—he went down low enough for his navigator to read the name through glasses. At the moment, it's still exclusive to me. And apart from you, Brett, that's how I'm going to keep it."

"So it's Marseilles next stop?" said Brett.

Dougal shook his head. "Not necessarily. They were still well out to sea. It could be anywhere along the Côte d'Azur. Marseilles, Toulon, Cannes, Nice. Or one of the smaller places."

"How are we going to find out which?" I asked and too late saw Brett's swift warning glance.

"You can leave that to me." Dougal gave a slow grin. "The dear old *Globe* has a long reach when it comes to a really gutsy story. There's a flight from here to Nice this afternoon, and I'll be on it, ready to shoot off to wherever it is that pair finally turn up."

"Brett!" I exclaimed. "We must be on that plane, too. Can you go and phone right away?"

From the look Dougal flashed me, I knew with a sinking heart that I'd been too eager. As Brett tried a second time to cover up for me, Dougal waved him down to silence.

"You called her Gail just now. Gail what, might I ask?"

Lifting his shoulders, Brett said carelessly, "It's Gail Fleming. Does it matter?"

Dougal's eyes widened with interest. "In other words, she's the niece! Brett, I thought we were buddies. You've been taking me for a ride!"

"You don't have to worry. I wasn't trying to steal your story."

"Maybe not, but you were sitting on an even bigger one." Dougal turned to me with a slow, confident smile. "Suppose I do the escorting from now on, Gail? I'll get you to see your uncle, on condition that I'm in on the meeting. But I want it exclusive, mind!"

"It's no go!" said Brett. "Gail stays with me."

"The only trouble is, Brett, that you won't know where Alexis Karel is unless I choose to tell you. And I'm not going to, not any more."

I said beseechingly, "Please, Dougal, don't you see, it would ruin everything if you were present. I've got to talk to my uncle privately. Given a chance, I'm sure I can persuade him to return home."

Brett weighed in too, pressuring Dougal out of friendship. It was an unfair tactic, and not unnaturally he resented it.

"You're asking the impossible," he said at one point. "You of all people ought to know that, Brett."

But in the end Dougal did agree to help us track down Alexis. And to keep the secret of my identity.

"Thanks," Brett said warmly. "I won't forget this."

Dougal made a sour face. "If my editor ever finds out what I've done, I won't be *allowed* to forget it."

He finished his coffee in one gulp and stood up to go. Then he hesitated, looking down on Brett and me.

"Bless you, my children," he said indulgently and strode off down the terrace steps, his jacket hitched over his shoulder.

Chapter Eight

It was five in the afternoon when Brett and I arrived at the Hôtel de l'Etoile in Nice. We checked in and went upstairs. At the door of my room, Brett paused and looked at me, his dark eyes lingering on my face.

"Gail, can I trust you not to run off again on your own? Dougal is really going out on a limb for you, so you'd better play it straight with him, even if you don't with me."

Remembering where my rash act of independence in Majorca had led me, I shivered.

"You needn't worry. I'm not moving an inch until we hear from Dougal. When do you think it'll be— this evening?"

"I've no idea. From what I could make out, that fishing boat Alexis hired is a slow old tub. You'll just have to be patient."

Left alone, I slid out of my coat and sank down on the bed, kicking off my shoes and drawing up my legs. I lay back, gazing out through the window at the hyacinth-blue Mediterranean sky.

All the way from Palma to Nice, I had scanned the sea far below us, wondering if I might catch a glimpse of the small boat that carried Alexis and Belle. But it was a vain hope. There were dozens of tiny craft upon the glittering water, any one of which could have been theirs. Or they might have been on a different course altogether.

Surely, though, they'd have to make landfall soon. But where? Brett and I were all set to make a quick dash to any point along the Riviera coastline the instant Dougal gave us the answer to that question. There was a car waiting for us downstairs in the hotel garage, a little Renault that Brett had hired at the airport.

The feeling of expectancy had me all tensed up and on edge, as if even a split second lost might prove vital.

I roused, startled by the sound of a knock on my door.

"Gail! It's me—Brett."

In a single moment I leaped up off the bed, running in stockinged feet to let him in. As I opened the door, a sudden wave of giddiness hit me, and I staggered. Brett shot out his arms to steady me.

"What's the matter? Aren't you well?"

"I'm all right," I snapped, furious with myself. "Have you heard something from Dougal?"

"No, not yet. But it's more than time we had some dinner."

I shook my head. "I don't feel like anything to eat."

"You've hardly had a thing since breakfast," he protested. "Gail, are you quite sure you're all right?"

His hands still held me by the shoulders, supporting me. Feeling suddenly self-conscious, I broke away and took a step back.

"I was lying down when you knocked, and I suppose I must have jumped up too quickly. I was a bit dizzy, that's all. I'm okay now."

"Then come and eat. I'll see you downstairs in ten minutes."

Brett had made the hotel reservation from Nice Airport because we needed to give Dougal a definite phone number where we could be reached in a hurry. Dougal was staying a few miles along the coast at Cannes, in a hotel where he'd often stayed before.

"It's just as well for us to separate," he'd said. "On a hot story like this, everyone's jumpy, suspecting everyone else of pulling a fast one. If we stick together, it might raise suspicions. Anyway, you two won't want me sticking so close to you."

The Hôtel de l'Etoile was very French, a superior family-type establishment to which I could imagine the same people returning year after year for their *vacances*. The staff tended to speak in murmurs, adding

to the general atmosphere of hush. The dining room
was ornately splendid in Empire style, dominated by
a pair of glittering crystal chandeliers.

The food was splendid, too, and I quickly found my
appetite. We ate a delicious sort of onion tart with
anchovies, and then pork cutlets. With it we drank a
rosé wine, light but quite heady. I found myself re-
laxing, my thoughts straying. Once upon a time, I reflected dreamily, Brett and I would really have en-
joyed eating in a place like this.

Brett was more relaxed, too. He smiled at me across
the table.

"Upstairs just now, I really thought you were going
to pass out on me. Gail, why don't you give up this
fool idea of finding Alexis? No one would blame you."

"Except myself! No, Brett, I've got to go on now
that I've come this far."

"Time was," he said bitterly, "when you'd have
listened to me."

Time was when I had loved him! When he could
do no wrong in my eyes—except to find another woman more attractive than I.

Brett must have seen the color creeping to my
cheeks. With a little dismissive shrug, he muttered
something under his breath. I wished I could ask him
what it was he'd said, but I didn't want to show him I
was curious.

After we'd had coffee in the salon, I went back upstairs to put through a call to Rudi. This time the connections were made quickly. Rudi answered at once,
as if he'd been waiting right beside the telephone.

"What's happening, Gail?"

"We've come to Nice. There's no doubt Alexis is
heading here. Any time now we expect to get news of
his arrival, and then I hope to see him. Rudi, how is
Madeleine?"

"She's been in low spirits today. It would be better
if you were here with her, Gail."

"She doesn't know anything, does she?" I asked in
sudden panic. "You haven't told her?"

"No, she knows nothing yet. But how much longer

can we hope to keep her in the dark? Give up and come home, Gail, and you and I will break it to Madeleine together."

I fingered the pale-blue damask of the bedspread, feeling painfully torn and undecided about what to do for the best.

"Rudi, I know how difficult it is for you, but please try and hold on just a little longer, just another day or so. You want to have this horrible business cleared up, don't you, as much as I do?"

"Of course I do, Gail! But we've got to think of Madeleine."

"I think of her all the time, Rudi," I said. "Give her my love, won't you? And look after her for me."

I went straight to bed. After the long hours of tension my body was greedy for sleep, and I dropped off almost at once.

It wasn't restful sleep, though. My mind was like a kaleidoscope full of changing patterns of faces. Alexis, looking directly at me but his eyes not quite meeting mine. Belle, her long copper-colored hair shaken loose and free, the sexily provocative Belle of the newspaper picture. Madeleine, pale and fragile, holding out her arms to me beseechingly and uttering a thin plaintive cry that I couldn't quite catch. And Rudi, his dark eyes concerned for me, a little anxious about the wisdom of what I was doing. Then Brett and Elspeth Vane, together in a close embrace, and Elspeth smiling at me over Brett's shoulder in supercilious triumph.

In my sleep, in my dreams, I began to shed bitter, hopeless tears.

I heard Brett calling my name, sharply, without gentleness. I felt him shaking me.

"Come on, Gail! Wake up. You're out like a log!"

My eyes flew open and I blinked, dazzled by the light of the bedside lamp. Brett was bending over me. He was fully dressed, carrying his sheepskin jacket.

"Your door was unlocked, so I came straight in. I've just had a call from Dougal." He broke off, peering at me closely. "Gail, you've been crying."

Impatiently, I brushed my tears away. "What's happened? Have they landed? Did Dougal tell you where . . . ?"

Brett nodded. "We're dead lucky—luckier than Dougal himself. They've turned up right here in Nice. *La Golondrina* berthed about a half hour ago, and Alexis and Belle have checked in at the Hôtel des Alpes-Maritimes!"

I was suddenly gripped with nervous excitement. I threw back the bed covers and swung my legs out. "What time is it?"

"About six A.M., so you'd better put something warm on. It'll be chilly out."

I went over to the washbasin for a hasty splash, expecting Brett to leave me alone. But he didn't move, and I was aware of his eyes watching me. I suddenly became self-conscious in my wispy nylon pajamas.

"I'll only be a minute," I said tersely. "If you'll just——"

"Wait outside?" Brett gave an amused shrug. "Okay, if you say so."

Hurriedly, I pulled on slacks and a white sweater. I flicked a comb through my hair and grabbed up my coat and handbag.

Brett was right outside the door. "That was quick. But then you never did hang about getting yourself ready, I remember. It was something I always——"

I chopped him off abruptly. "Where is this Hôtel des Alpes-Maritimes?"

"It's one of those enormous places along the Promenade des Anglais. Those two certainly like living it up."

The garage of our hotel was at the rear of the building. It was by no means full, but to my dismay we found a big black Citröen parked so that it blocked the exit of our hired Renault.

"Damn!" exclaimed Brett. "We'll have to shift this brute before we can get out."

I was in a fever to be moving. "Hadn't we better forget about the car and walk, Brett?"

"No, it's quite a distance. This shouldn't take a moment." Brett went around the Citröen, trying each of the door handles in turn. They were all locked.

"I don't mind walking," I persisted. "Or perhaps we can find a taxi."

"No, you wait here a minute, and I'll go and fetch the night porter. He'll be able to help."

It seemed an eternity that Brett left me there in the semi-darkness of the garage, lit by just one light at the far end. I was so on edge that my eyes started imagining menacing shapes in the gloomy recesses, and I shivered. This was the final moment of my quest. In a matter of minutes I would know the truth about Alexis. I would discover once and for all what sort of man my uncle really was.

At last I heard the echoing sound of footsteps. More lights were turned on, and Brett appeared with a short, tubby little man who wore steel-rimmed glasses.

Tutting to himself, the porter repeated Brett's tour of the Citröen door handles, refusing to take our word that they were all locked. When convinced, he produced an enormous bunch of keys and started trying them each in turn, methodically.

He could not understand it, he muttered. The gentleman who owned this car always parked it over there in the corner. Not here. And anyway, he never locked it. But perhaps last night he was a little . . .

Maddened by the man's slowness, I had to watch while he inserted one key after another. He must have tried at least twenty-five before the lock gave a click. He turned to us and beamed as he opened the door.

"*Voilà!*"

With the handbrake off, the two men started to push the big, heavy car clear of ours. I threw in my own weight to hurry things along. Then Brett fished in his pocket for a tip.

"Oh, come on!" I said. "For heaven's sake!"

"A few seconds isn't going to make any difference," Brett reproved me.

At this hour of the morning it was still dark, and the streets were almost deserted. In only a few moments we were driving along the broad Promenade des Anglais, with the long curving line of street lamps tracing the huge sweep of the bay, mile after mile of tropical palms and luxuriant flower beds.

The Hôtel des Alpes-Maritimes had a colonnade of white pillars the entire length of its façade. Of the hundreds upon hundreds of windows, most were in darkness.

Brett swung into the forecourt and found a place to park.

We pushed through glass revolving doors into a vast shadowed entrance hall that was like a Byzantine palace of marble and mosaic under a lofty vaulted ceiling. In the pool of bright light around the reception desk a group of men were talking excitedly among themselves.

Brett took one look at them and halted. "Damn! They've beaten us to it, Gail!"

"What do you mean?"

"They're newspapermen, that's what!"

"Oh no!" I cried in dismay. "But how could they know? And so quickly!" Dougal had seemed confident that no one else knew about Alexis's plans.

"These chaps have an uncanny instinct when there's a good story," said Brett. "Come on, we'll just have to bluff it out."

Seizing my hand, he thrust his way through the bunch of reporters to the desk, pulling me after him. He addressed the *concierge* in a brisk, commanding voice.

"The number of Dr. Karel's room, please. Dr. Alexis Karel."

"I regret, *monsieur,* but you must wait with the others."

The man was enjoying to the hilt his brief moment of power. "Dr. Karel has agreed to receive the press in half an hour."

"Oh, but we're not reporters," I said impulsively. "We want to see Dr. Karel on a private matter."

The hush that fell upon the group of newsmen was something tangible. Six pairs of eyes all turned to stare at me. Dimly, I heard the *concierge's* impatient voice. "Dr. Karel will see no one until he is ready, *madame.*

Those are his precise instructions. He is angry at being hounded by newspapers in this way."

Someone took a step toward me, a middle-aged gray-haired man who looked as if he'd dressed in as great a hurry as I had.

"Hey, miss, what d'you want to see Alexis Karel about?"

"The same as you," said Brett quickly before I could speak. "You know how it is—we thought it was worth a try."

"That's Brett Warrender," someone muttered, and another voice asked, "Who's the bird with him?"

"Hands off her!" said Brett lightly. "She belongs to me."

A whisper came from the back of the group and caught me like a whiplash. My name!

It was picked up at once. "Gail Fleming? Say, isn't that Karel's niece?"

There was a blinding blue-white flash and then another. I heard the click of camera shutters and held up my hands to shield my face. The reporters pressed around me purposefully.

"Miss Fleming, maybe you can tell us . . ."

I was saved by a sudden commotion from somewhere behind them. A new voice called out excitedly, "What do you know—Karel's skipped out again! I just got it from the floor waiter. Him and that doll he's with —checked out, bags and all, five minutes ago."

Chapter Nine

Brett and I were suddenly left alone near the reception desk as the reporters surged away toward the new-comer, arguing noisily among themselves.

I felt the hard grip of Brett's fingers on my wrist. "Come on, Gail—now's our chance!" He waved a banknote at the bewildered *concierge*. "Quick, get us out of here without that lot knowing."

The man caught on fast. In a couple of seconds we were being shepherded through the private office and out of a door at the rear into a long, dimly lit corridor.

Brett slid out a second banknote and held it up between his finger and thumb.

"Do you know where Dr. Karel is heading? Where he's gone?"

"Monsieur, I know nothing. My instructions were exactly as I told you. All arrangements must have been made with the manager personally. Perhaps he could—"

"There's no time for that," said Brett. "We've got to get out of here before they catch on that we've gone."

We emerged into a dark courtyard. Brett was still gripping me by the wrist.

"It must be this way around to the front," he muttered. "I hope to God those press boys won't have come out yet."

We were in luck. When we reached the forecourt, we were within a few yards of where the Renault was parked. There were no reporters in sight. We made a quick dash to the car and were away in a moment, swinging out onto the promenade, heading back the way we had come.

Brett said grimly, "I don't think anyone saw us. Have a look and see if any car tried to follow."

I craned my neck to peer out of the rear window. The only vehicle in sight was a small truck.

"No, I think we're in the clear."

I felt sick at heart. To think that I'd been so near to Alexis, missing him by just a few minutes! If only, I thought despondently, we'd not had that holdup getting the car out of the garage, then we might have been in time. We might have reached the Hôtel des Alpes-Maritimes before the gathering reporters had driven Alexis away.

I said, puzzled, "I still don't see how those newspapermen could have tracked Alexis down so quickly."

"These things happen, Gail—there's nothing so surprising about it. The press world is geared to acting fast on information received, and all manner of people give them tipoffs in return for a small handout. Hotel staff, taxi drivers—it could have been anyone." He shrugged his shoulders. "If only Alexis realized, he's *asking* for publicity by staying at these deluxe places. Sitting up and begging for it! If he just had the sense to choose somewhere a shade less flashy, he'd stand a chance of getting by unnoticed. Now he's had to escape from the press again, and we're back to square one."

"And those reporters know about *me*," I said miserably.

"That fact hadn't escaped my notice, either," Brett said with withering sarcasm. "In the future you'd better watch your tongue."

Brett was driving fast along the promenade, and I noticed that he shot past the turn that led back to our hotel.

"Where are you going?" I asked.

"Somewhere quiet so we can stop and think out what to do next."

"Why not go back to the Etoile?"

He didn't try to hide his scorn. "Grow up, Gail! You just said yourself that those newsmen know about you. How long do you imagine it will take them to track down where Gail Fleming is staying in Nice? If some of them aren't around at the Hôtel de l'Etoile within minutes, waiting to pounce on you, I'd be amazed. It's the one place we mustn't go to right now."

"But all our things are there!"

"Hard luck! That's the least of our worries at the moment. Unless . . ." he glanced at me hopefully, "unless you're ready to drop this half-baked scheme of yours and go back home like a sensible girl."

"How can I, now?" I said unhappily. "How could I ever admit to Madeleine that I got so near Alexis and then just gave up?"

"You needn't ever tell her."

Brett swung away from the seafront by some formally laid-out gardens and headed into the town. As we approached an intersection, the traffic lights changed to red and Brett pulled up. Alongside us, a big black car slid to a halt. Brett was staring straight ahead through the windshield, his fingers impatiently tapping the rim of the steering wheel. In the light of the street-lamp I could see the clean, sharp angles of his face. His mouth was set hard.

Something beyond his profile caught my eye, something in the black car. A cascade of gleaming copper-colored hair.

The shock was like a blow in the chest. At that same moment the woman turned her head to glance out of the window, casually at first, then with an abrupt jerk. Our eyes met point-blank. There was no possible doubt left—it was Belle Forsyth!

I caught my breath and clutched at Brett's arm.

"Look, there they are!"

The lights changed to green, and the black car surged forward. Through its rear window I could see Alexis at the wheel, the pure white of his hair. And beside him, Belle had turned in her seat to look back at us.

"Get after them, Brett! Please hurry!"

He reacted at once, stamping down his foot so that I felt myself pressed back into the seat.

"Are you really certain, Gail?"

"Yes, I *saw* them. Belle was looking straight at me."

"Do you think she recognized you?"

"I know she did! It was just as big a shock to her as it was to me."

"I'll bet!"

We were a hundred yards behind them, and Belle still seemed to be looking back at us. Surely she must have told Alexis that she'd seen me, yet there was no sign of his slowing down. In fact he was still accelerating.

A coldness ran through my body at the thought that he might deliberately be evading me. How *could* Alexis do that after our closeness to each other?

But *had* Belle told him that she'd seen me? She wouldn't want Alexis to stop and talk to me, knowing that I would try my best to persuade him to come back to England, come back to Madeleine. If *I* believed that I stood a chance with Alexis, then perhaps Belle believed it, too. Perhaps she was not altogether confident of her hold on him.

"Can't you go any faster?" I urged Brett.

"Have a heart! It's a damn great Cadillac they've got! Our only hope is more traffic lights or some hold-up."

But our luck had run out. The Cadillac swept ahead of us unimpeded through the early-morning streets, until the buildings thinned out and we were beginning to climb.

"We don't stand a chance of catching them now, Gail. I reckon I know where they're heading—up to the Grand Corniche road. They'll just leave us standing."

"Don't give up, Brett," I begged. "Please!"

The distant tail lights of the Cadillac seemed to blink, and then they were gone. We reached the bend ourselves, took it fast, and we could see the lights again, higher up, the gap between us wider. Brett coaxed our puny little car up the brutally steep gradient of the winding Corniche road. Occasionally, headlights of other cars rocketed toward us, half blinding us. And each time when they'd gone past and our eyes had recovered, the winking red lights of the Cadillac seemed a little farther away, until there was no sign of them at all in the darkness ahead.

"Maybe they'll stop for some reason or other," I said without real hope. "There's always a chance."

"Why in hell should they stop? Alexis's one idea is to get away from you."

"No!" I protested. "I can't believe that. I don't believe Belle told him she'd seen us."

"Then why did he drive through Nice like a bat out of hell, trying to shake us off?"

I needed an explanation of that myself. Eventually

I hit on one that seemed plausible.

"Belle might not have told him it was *us* on their tail. She might have said that we were reporters. She wouldn't want Alexis to stop and give me a chance of talking to him."

"You've got a point there," Brett acknowledged grudgingly.

He continued driving, but I could tell it was only a token gesture, just to satisfy me that he was doing his best. After another ten minutes or so he drew onto the side and cut the engine.

"We might as well face it—we've lost them. So we'd better decide what to do now. Give up, Gail, that's my advice."

I didn't answer him. After a moment, I said, "Will Dougal still be willing to help us, do you think?"

"Dougal must be hopping mad at this moment. He thought he'd got an exclusive, and by now he'll have found out that the story is blown."

"But he can't blame *us* for that."

"Let's hope not. We'll have to see."

We had climbed very high. In these last moments before sunrise, the sea seemed to glow with an opalescent sheen, broken by bars of shadow. Far below a few pinpricks of light marked a small town somewhere along the coast. A car flashed past us on the road, but when the sound of its engine had faded there was only silence.

I thought of all the other times that Brett and I had stopped by the roadside at some quiet spot. Now, in the little Renault, he and I were sitting very close but not quite touching—carefully not touching. Yet I had never been more aware of him. I had never felt more dependent on him. I was conscious of that faint elusive redolence that makes up a man—this one special man. A subtle blend impossible to define, the warm male smell of him.

Nervously I edged away another inch and instantly experienced a curious sense of chill.

Brett said thoughtfully, "What we need is a hideout.

Somewhere that's safe from reporters, but with a phone so we can keep in touch with Dougal. And I think I know just the place."

"Where, Brett?" I asked eagerly.

"It's not far from here, up in the hills toward the Italian border. A couple of friends of mine have a small house there—an old *mas* they've had renovated. There's not a neighbor within miles. They're the kind who like to get away from it all."

I felt dubious. "But, Brett, we can't land ourselves on them just like that! I mean, if they like peace and quiet . . ."

"Leave it all to me," he said confidently, starting the car. "Let's drive on until we find a café, and we'll have some breakfast. Then as soon as it's a reasonable hour to get civilized people from their beds, I'll give the Shackletons a ring."

Against reason, perhaps, I felt a surge of new hope. I had actually seen Alexis, and the more I thought about it, the more convinced I became that Belle hadn't told him about seeing me. It was a theory that made sense. Comforting, encouraging sense. Belle Forsyth was *afraid* of letting me talk to my uncle.

The sun was coming up now. Under the shadow of the mountains it was still dark, but the sky was paling to an oyster gray, touched in the east with the faintest brushing of rose. Far out to sea the first rays of sunlight were glinting upon the water.

As we drove on, I watched color come back to the world, the clear vivid colors of Provence. Dark burnt orange from sun-baked earth, every shade of green and gray from the trees that hugged the slopes, the white of almond blossom and the sharp spicy yellow of mimosa. And there were bushes of some waxy-looking coral flowers that I didn't recognize. It all stood out in high relief, glowing against the early-morning purity of the sky, the deep cobalt blue of the sea.

Soon we reached a little town called La Turbie, and Brett found somewhere to park.

"I suppose you don't want to look over the Roman

ruins," he said. "There's a spot where you get a fantastic view of Monte Carlo. Especially at night, with all the lights."

"You've been here before, then?"

"A few times. We were here in the summer, filming."

We! Bleakly, I thought of Brett with Elspeth Vane. She was a woman suited to the glittering life of the Côte d'Azur. Monte Carlo, Nice, St. Tropez . . . World sophisticates both of them, she and Brett.

Suddenly I became conscious of what I must look like at this moment. My clothes, straight out of a suitcase, dragged on in a rush. No time to do my hair properly or make up my face.

I opened the car door and put a foot to the ground. "Didn't you say something about breakfast?"

"Yes, sure. Let's go and find someplace."

A couple of minutes' walk through the streets of the ancient town, and we came to an attractive little café with gay orange awnings. Table and chairs were set out in front. But at this altitude, at this time of day, it was too cold to sit in the open, so we went inside. Brett ordered coffee and croissants from the incredibly handsome, dark young waiter, who looked Italian rather than French.

While we waited, Brett said musingly, "God knows where that pair are going to turn up next. There are places dotted all over Europe just as eligible as Palma and Nice."

My mind was still occupied with thinking about Elspeth—Elspeth and Brett. I said stupidly, "What do you mean by eligible?"

"Smart enough—fancy enough. It's the grand style he's been going for, isn't it? Staying at the ritziest hotels he can find."

I focused my attention. "Yes, that's what I can't understand. It's so completely unlike Alexis to be ostentatious."

"Men change, Gail. Or perhaps Alexis was like that underneath all the time." He shot me a tentative look. "It could be Belle's price, you know—living it up in the millionaires' playgrounds."

"Belle's price?"

Brett drew his thumbnail across the starched checked tablecloth, making a thin rasping sound.

"Gail, you've only seen Belle Forsyth as the capable, devoted nurse-companion to Madeleine. Being a man, I was shown a different side of her character. When Belle took her hair down she could be devastatingly sexy. It was enough to make any man—"

"Not Alexis!" But a faint note of doubt had crept into my voice.

"*Any* man," Brett insisted. "If it was not for the fact that Belle isn't my type, who knows?"

"Then what is your type?" I threw back at him and instantly regretted it.

When Brett looked at me it seemed that a shutter had dropped across his eyes. "You know the answer to that, Gail, don't you?"

Yes, I knew! We were back to Elspeth again.

Brett inquired if he could use the telephone. He was shown through a curtained archway at the back, and I heard a door close.

There was a sleepy hush upon the place. The only other customer, a fat, elderly man in a black beret, was studying his newspaper with deep concentration. Was he perhaps reading about Alexis? I wondered. Behind the counter, the handsome waiter was polishing glasses and kept glancing up at his reflection in a mirror. A huge, sleek tortoise-shell cat lay in a patch of sunlight by the window, lazily licking a paw. He eyed me impassively for a moment, yawned, stretched, and settled at once to sleep.

In less than five minutes Brett was back.

"All fixed, Gail. We're to take some food for ourselves, though—the Shackletons aren't prepared for unexpected guests at this time of year, and it's a long way to the shops."

"Brett, are you sure they don't mind?"

He shook his head. "I've known Bill Shackleton ever since we were at Cambridge together. He writes scripts for television nowadays, and Harriet writes those madly successful children's books. They're a great pair."

"What did you tell them about us? How much did you explain?"

"What about leaving the organizing to me, Gail? Make a big effort and trust me for once."

I flushed. "There's no need to be sarcastic."

Brett smiled at me with maddening condescension. "Drink up your coffee like a good girl, and we'll go and find an *épicerie* and buy some food. I don't know how long we're going to be holed up, but we'd better take enough for a couple of days or so."

"How about letting Dougal know where we'll be?"

He gave me a withering look. "Bread and cheese, eggs, ham, some fruit and coffee—how's that? And wine."

"I suppose so."

The thought of food didn't interest me at all. I wasn't looking forward to the prospect of maybe two days' complete inaction. But I had to go along with Brett's plan, because I knew that without him I'd get nowhere. Without Brett's help, I wouldn't have a hope of catching up with Alexis.

Chapter Ten

We were climbing higher all the time, thrusting deeper into the mountains. The road wound its way through a narrow gorge, just a rim on the edge of a seemingly vertical rockface. At one point we had to cross the ravine by a slender metal bridge that looked as if it would scarcely bear the weight of the car. Then at once we plunged into a dark tunnel where Brett needed to use the headlights.

We emerged into a different world—a harshly arid world that had its own sort of grandeur. The wide, parched valley was encircled by distant peaks, some crested with snow. Nearer, huge outcrops of limestone rock, blindingly white, stood out like jagged scars.

Here and there was a single olive tree, its contorted branches still winter-bare, and clusters of stunted pine shivered in the wind. In the hollows, where the sun could not penetrate, lay patches of crusted snow.

I shuddered at such bleakness. Yet people lived here, somehow scratching themselves a livelihood. We passed through a village, no more than a scattering of tumbledown houses. It seemed deserted, but I sensed eyes peering secretively from behind curtains.

Beyond the village the road divided, and Brett stopped to consult the map he'd bought in La Turbie. With the engine switched off, I could hear the wind sighing through the telephone wires beside the road. It was a mournful sound.

"We take the right fork here," said Brett, refolding the map. "It's not far now. How does the thought of a blazing log fire strike you?"

"Great!" I hugged closer into my coat. "I suppose it's very beautiful, Brett, but . . ."

He laughed. "That's the whole idea, isn't it? Nobody's going to think of looking for us in this wilderness."

Fifteen minutes later we came to a rough track leading off to the right. A mailbox was nailed to a pole, with a hand-painted sign beneath it: La Retraite.

"This is it," said Brett and swung onto the track. We bumped our way along for nearly a mile, twisting and turning. Pine trees blocked our view of the house until we were almost upon it.

La Retraite was a huddled mass of stone, crouching low upon the ground. The walls, the roof pantiles, the tufty grass around it were the same tawny gray. If I'd expected a welcome, I was disappointed. No figure stood in the doorway, no smoke curled from the squat chimney. The windows were tightly shuttered.

"Brett, are you quite sure this is the right place?"

"Of course I am."

"It . . . it looks so deserted. All shut up."

Brett made no comment as he stopped the car on the square of roughly leveled ground. For a moment or two he sat behind the wheel, making no move to get out. Then he said briskly, "Come on, let's have a look around."

There was still no sign of life from the house. I expected Brett to knock at the door, but instead he poked about in a crevice between two stones in the wall and withdrew a large and rusty iron key. He thrust it in the lock and without a backward glance at me opened the door and stepped inside.

"Brett," I began, "ought we to . . . ?"

"Come on in, Gail. We'd better get a fire going right away. It's like an icebox!"

Inside, with the shutters up, it was dark. I could see very little except that we were in a large oblong room, its flagstone floor partly covered by wool rugs. It felt bitterly cold, the raw cold of a house long empty.

"There's no one here!" I said, dismayed. Then suddenly I understood and swung around on Brett accusingly. "You knew there'd be nobody here, didn't you? There couldn't have been when you were supposed to be phoning. This place hasn't been lived in for ages."

"Not since autumn, actually," he agreed. "Bill and Harriet just spend the summer here. They say it's the only place they can escape and get some work done. Luckily for us, it's essential that the TV people can reach Bill quickly, or there'd be no phone." I heard a ting as he lifted the receiver. "Yes, it's working, so we'll be all right."

"You've got a nerve! You told me they——"

"Keep cool, Gail. I had to spin you a yarn. I knew you wouldn't have come at all if you'd known the Shackletons weren't here."

"Too true I wouldn't! And I'm not staying, either. You'd better think again, Brett."

His voice reached me out of the gloom. Calm and reasonable. "There's nowhere else as safe as this, Gail. Give me one good reason why we shouldn't stay."

"There are all sorts of reasons. The Shackletons, for one thing. What would they think if they knew you were making use of their place like this?"

"Bill and Harriet wouldn't care a damn. They've often told me that if I ever wanted somewhere quiet to go when I was on the coast, I could always come here. How else do you imagine I knew where the key was hidden?"

I was silent. There ought to be something I could say, some retort that would crush Brett's unbearable self-assurance. But I couldn't think of it.

He laughed softly. "Don't tell me you're having an attack of frozen virtue. I thought you and I had got past that stage long ago."

I felt my cheeks flame and was grateful it was too dark for him to see.

"We'll freeze to death if we don't get a fire going," said Brett, suddenly practical. "I'll nip outside and open up the shutters, then I'll fetch in some logs. There's always a pile kept around at the back. Look and see if you can find some paper and kindling wood."

Searching, I discovered the full extent of the *mas*, and it wasn't much. Opening off the living room was a room with a large double bed. I shut the door quickly, wondering about sleeping arrangements. The tiny lean-to kitchen contained a shallow stone sink with no taps, a contraption that looked like a primitive oil stove, a cupboard with cleaning things, and a larder that was bare except for, on the bottom shelf, the very things I wanted.

I had paper and sticks piled ready in the grate when Brett came back with an armful of split logs. In about three minutes the fire was roaring up the wide-throated chimney. With the sun coming in through the open shutters, the room began to look more cheerful. I was forced to admit that it possessed a certain charm.

It was furnished very simply, the walls painted white, the floor rugs and curtains in strong bright colors —orange, lime green and yellow. There was a circular dining table of natural pine and four matching ladder-back chairs, a deep, soft couch with a scattering of cushions, which Brett dragged around to face the fire.

He disappeared outside again and returned with the carton of food we'd bought, the two long French loaves sticking out of the top.

"I think an early lunch is indicated, don't you, Gail? What do you say to canned soup? I fancy kidney myself, followed by some of that nice ripe Camembert. And we'll break open a bottle of the Chablis."

With the warmth of the fire beginning to penetrate my frozen bones, and the prospect of food, I was feeling mellowed, more human. I suddenly realized that I was devastatingly hungry. I'd scarcely eaten any breakfast.

I followed Brett through to the kitchen, leaving the door wide open to take some of the fire's heat with us.

"I'll see to it, Brett. That is, if I can manage the oil stove."

"It's not difficult once it knows who's boss. I'll show you. Then I'll get a bucket of water from the hand pump, which incidentally doubles as the bathroom."

"Bathroom! I could just do with . . ."

Brett grinned maliciously. "You strip and crouch under the spout while somebody pumps for you. Bill and Harriet swear by it. They say it's most invigorating. Care to try?"

"Thanks, I'll do without. Look, Brett, hadn't you better phone Dougal before we do anything else?"

"I've done it already, from the café."

"When you were supposed to be ringing here and fixing it with the Shackletons." On an impulse, I added, "I'm sorry for being bitchy, Brett. You're doing your best to help me, and heaven knows why you should."

He smiled at me briefly. Or perhaps it was a rueful smile against himself.

"I was dead lucky and caught Dougal just as he got back to his hotel in Cannes. He was flaming mad about his exclusive story going bust, but he's promised that he'll ring us at this number as soon as he hears anything more."

After we had eaten, I heated some water and washed the dishes, then returned to the couch to relax and let the fire soak into me. There was nothing I

could do, no action I could take. Until Dougal phoned
with fresh news, I would just have to curb my impatience and wait. In fact, this brief respite from rush
and activity was rather delicious.

I drifted into a light doze, conscious of Brett moving
around the room, doing this and that. In the end, I fell
deeply asleep.

The sound of the door being closed aroused me.
Opening my eyes, I saw that Brett had just come in
from outside. The fire was a glow of red embers, and I
realized the daylight was fading.

"What time is it?" I asked drowsily.

He flicked his wrist in a gesture that I'd seen him
make a hundred times before. "Just on five-fifteen.
You had a good sleep. You must have needed it."

I snapped wide awake. "Hasn't Dougal phoned yet?
It's *hours* since we got here."

"He will—the second there's anything to tell us. But
it may be that Alexis has really gone to ground this
time."

"Oh no! You don't really think that, do you, Brett?"

He shrugged. "It might be best all around if he
vanished, considering the trouble he's causing everyone. Just now, while you were asleep, I was thinking
what a terrible fraud that man is. I remembered the
touching little gathering at Deer's Leap on Christmas
Eve. Both families gathered around the fire, with the
radio tuned to the BBC European service to hear Alexis
giving his annual message of hope and comfort to his
fellow countrymen. The famous Wenceslas Message!
At the end, my father was so moved that he couldn't
speak for a minute. There were actually tears in the
old chap's eyes as he silently produced the bottle of
slivovice he'd bought specially for the occasion. Oh, it
makes me sick!"

I bit my lip, keeping back tears. Being in the United
States, I had missed Christmas at Deer's Leap this year,
but it was always the same. A solemn ritual. Alexis had
broadcast the Wenceslas Message each Christmas Eve
since his escape to freedom.

Brett went on in the same bitter voice, "It's all very

fine you having this crazy idea of talking Alexis around and making him see the error of his ways—but I doubt if *I* will ever forgive him. And I reckon that goes for a great many people."

Out of my despair came a flash of anger. "You shouldn't be so quick to pass judgment. What right have you to condemn Alexis before you've heard his side of the story?"

Brett's dark eyes were flinty. "Look who's talking about fairness! I never remember *you* being ready to give *me* the benefit of the doubt."

I almost snapped back at him, but I checked myself in time. There was no use in our bickering, no sense in fighting past battles again and reopening old wounds. A log fell to the stone hearth with a crash of sparks, and it gave me an excuse to kneel down and attend to the fire.

Later, for supper, I made a large ham omelet, using Harriet Shackleton's heavy iron skillet. We had more of the Camembert and some grapes to follow. Brett opened another bottle of wine.

We sat opposite each other at the round table, in the pool of light cast by a figured brass oil lamp. My mind leaped back across the months. It had often been like this in my apartment in London—just the two of us in a softly lit room.

But it was different now. Everything was changed. Brett and I sat and made polite talk, empty words and phrases strung together. Whenever a possible danger point loomed, we both drew back hastily into the safety of platitudes.

Brett got up from the table and began to prowl about the room restlessly. He seemed just as much on edge as I was.

"The moon's up," he said, stopping by the window and drawing aside the curtain. "It looks beautiful. Get your coat on, Gail, and we'll go outside for a few minutes."

The wind had dropped and the air was crisp. The moon was low in the sky, just a half circle, and its pure clear light made a landscape of vivid contrasts. The distant snow-capped peaks were etched silver against an indigo sky, while nearby a massive outcrop of rock rose like a miniature mountain, the limestone glowing a translucent bluish white. The shadows were deep, black, mysterious.

Brett said, pointing, "I remember there's a path leading around that big crag. From the farther side you get a terrific view right down the entire length of the valley. It's fantastic!"

"Can we go and look?"

"Not now. The path is too narrow to be safe at night, even when there's a moon. Besides, one of us must stay close to the phone. If we're still here in the morning, you can go and have a look then."

The cold was striking through my coat, but I had no urge to go back inside. Not yet. There was a strange enchantment about this silent, silver world of moonlight. Nothing seemed quite real. I felt a fluttering within me that was almost panic.

It plucked a chord of memory. Some time, some place, this had happened to me before. Suddenly, I recalled the occasion vividly—the Ivory Room at Deer's Leap, when I had met Brett again after an interval of more than ten years. That evening I had experienced this same curious sensation, as if everything was without substance and I was floating adrift, drowning, having no say in my own destiny.

I shivered, from the cold, from the remembrance. Brett's fingers reached out to me, and I let my hand stay in his. It seemed so natural, so utterly right. The misty vapor of our breathing mingled and hung in a little cloud, scarcely moving in the stillness of the night.

I don't remember if there was a moment of decision. I only remember going into Brett's arms, being held, clinging to him. I remember the feel of his lips on mine —ice-cold, then warm.

"Gail," he murmured softly. "Darling Gail."

Without any more words being spoken, as if the silence was somehow too precious to break, we turned

and went back inside. Brett tossed logs onto the fire,
and I stood very still, watching him, watching the
golden, leaping flames, conscious of the flames that
leaped within me.

There were no explanations, no apologies, no forgiveness. That night it was as if Brett and I had never
been apart.

Chapter Eleven

This time when I awoke, the fire had almost died, but
the room still felt warm from the glowing embers and
the stored-up heat of the massive hearthstone. The
lamp had burned itself out, leaving a slight tang of
kerosene in the air. Around the edges of the curtains
the first gray light of morning was showing.

I had spent the night on the couch, wrapped in
blankets, cushions under my head. Brett lay within
touch of my outstretched fingers, rolled in more blankets on the hearthrug. He seemed to be deeply asleep,
not even stirring when I leaned down and drew back
the blankets so that I could see the luminous dial of his
wristwatch.

Five minutes to eight! Over twenty-four hours had
gone by, and still no further news of Alexis. The realization wiped away my exalted mood of the night.
Yesterday's problems were still with me, I thought
bleakly.

I rose from the couch and went out to the freezing
kitchen, washing as best I could in icy water. I longed
for a good hot bath and clean clothes.

I considered whether to start getting breakfast but
decided not to. Brett might as well have his sleep un-
disturbed.

I went back to the living room and stood for a moment looking down at him, feeling my heartbeat quick-
en. He lay on his back with his head turned to one
side, so that I saw the outline of his profile, the firm

contours of his neck and shoulder. I had an urge to sink down on my knees and fondle his tousled dark-brown hair.

I made myself move away. After a moment, I slipped on my coat and went quietly to the door, letting myself out.

It was an overcast morning, the distant peaks cut off from view by banks of snow clouds, slate-gray and threatening. Hands thrust deeply into the pockets of my coat, I paced moodily along the track that led to the road, while I thought about Brett. Last night, what had it meant? Nothing had really changed; there was still the question of Elspeth. Brett had made me no promises. He had shown no regret for the time we had been apart, those long wasted months. Perhaps last night had been just an interlude for him, without any feeling of commitment. Perhaps he had merely taken what he sensed I was only too eager to give. My face burned as I recalled how easy I had made it for him.

And yet, how insistent he had been to come with me on my quest for Alexis. He had done everything possible to help me, taking me on a trail I could never have followed alone.

Why had he done all this?

Last night I believed I had found the answer. But the cold gray light of morning, the cold light of reason, told me it was only wishful thinking.

Why, then?

Ahead, the track ran through the clump of pine trees. It looked dark in there and somehow ominous. With a shudder, I turned back.

Retracing my steps, I came to where a path led off to the right, curving away toward the massive limestone crag. I remembered that Brett had spoken of a viewpoint from the farther side. This wasn't really the morning for distant views, but I might be able to see something. And it would kill time.

On my left, the scrubby ground fell away sharply. The path, like a corniche road in miniature, followed every convolution of the clifflike rockface. Soon, I found myself on a ledge only a couple of feet wide.

I walked on, perfectly confident, until suddenly I felt my foot slip under me. It wasn't much but enough to unnerve me. Looking down, I saw there were patches of frozen snow on the path, almost invisible against the white of the limestone.

I decided it would be foolish to go on and risk a bad fall. On a narrow path like this I could so easily slip over the edge. Even at this point the drop was about fifteen feet, and farther along it looked considerably more, sheer to jagged rocks below.

As I turned to go back, I heard a slight noise from somewhere above me. It sounded like a scrabble of small loose stones.

I paused to listen. A bird? But I'd seen and heard no birds this morning. Some small animal, perhaps? I had a vague idea that chamois were to be found in this part of Provence. Or it could be something as ordinary as a rabbit.

After a few moments when the only break in the silence was the sighing of the wind through the pine trees, I started to move again. But at once I jerked to a halt, really startled. This time the sound I heard was quite different. A human voice. A cry of distress. Faint, muffled, but unmistakably a man's voice.

"Help! Help!"

I stared up at the rockface above me, wondering what to do. It was very steep and looked dangerously crumbly. And anyway, I couldn't be sure whether the cry had come from up there or farther along toward the end of the crag.

"Where are you?" I cried.

"Here."

It sounded fainter than before and definitely seemed to come from farther on.

I started along the path but almost at once slipped again on the ice and realized I would have to take care.

"I'm coming!" I called out. "As quickly as I can."

"Hurry! For God's sake, hurry."

He sounded close to exhaustion. Despite the danger,

© Lorillard 1975

Hello Max.

The maximum 120mm cigarette.

Great tobaccos. Terrific taste.
And a long, lean,
<u>all-white</u> dynamite look.

Menthol or Regular.

"Hello long, lean and delicious."

MAX

MAX

MENTHOL 120's by KENT

FILTER 120's by KENT

Regular: 17 mg.
"tar," 1.3 mg.
nicotine; Menthol:
8 mg. "tar," 1.3
mg. nicotine av.
er cigarette by
TC Method.

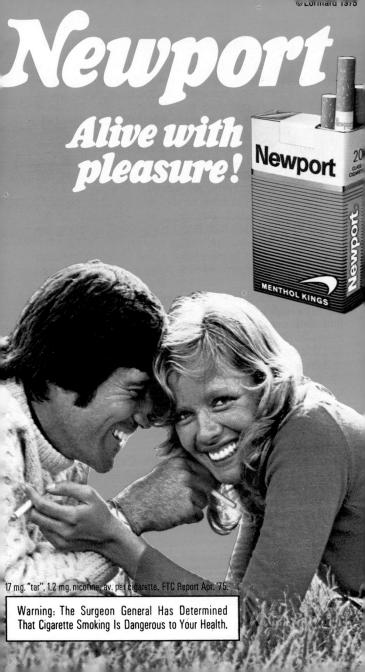

© Lorillard 1975

Newport

Alive with pleasure!

Newport
20
CLASS
CIGARETTES

Newport®

MENTHOL KINGS

17 mg. "tar", 1.2 mg. nicotine, av. per cigarette, FTC Report Apr. '75.

Warning: The Surgeon General Has Determined
That Cigarette Smoking Is Dangerous to Your Health.

I put on an extra spurt, trailing a hand against the rough rock wall as an illusion of support. Then suddenly my foot trod ice again and skidded from under me. My fingers clutched wildly, frantically, but there was nothing to grip. I was slipping over the edge, falling into empty space. I felt my head hit rock with a crack, and momentarily I blacked out.

It was a bush that had saved me. A spiny, prickly, half-dead bush, growing from a crevice in the rock. I'd clung to it instinctively, desperately. Dazed, I looked up and saw that the edge of the path was two or three feet above my head. But the instant I moved in an effort to reach it, the dry twiggy bush I clung to cracked ominously. Stretching out my leg, I found a tiny foothold, but it gave way when I tried it, sending down a shower of crumbled rock as a chastening warning.

I tried to keep calm, to make myself think. Clutching my slender support, I scanned the face of the rock and took careful note. There was another crack within reach of my left foot. Gingerly, I pushed in my toe and this time it held.

The bush, relieved of my weight as I let go, sprang up and tore at my face. With a reaching grabbing movement, I got a hand over the edge. Then, laboriously, terrified every moment that I would lose my grip, I hauled myself upward. It seemed an eternity before I was safely back on the path.

Crouched on my knees, I remained motionless for several seconds, breathing heavily. It was a miracle to be alive.

At last I stood up. The wind seemed to be rising, and a few tiny flakes of snow whirled by. I listened, but I heard no repetition of the cry for help.

I was in no state now to offer help to anyone. But I couldn't stand here doing nothing. I had to rouse Brett, quickly. I started back along the path, stumbling, terrified every second of another fall.

But before I came within sight of the house I heard him calling me.

"Gail! Gail, where are you?"

"I'm here!" I shouted in relief. "Here on the path."

I stood still, waiting for him to come. As he appeared around the curve, he stopped and stared at me in astonishment.

"What the devil!"

"Oh, Brett!" I gasped and flung myself into his arms.

"Darling, what's happened? You look in a terrible mess, your slacks torn and your coat all smeared with dirt!"

"I fell. But there's no time to tell you about it now. Brett, I heard someone calling for help!"

"You what!"

"It was a man. He sounded dreadfully weak. He must be in real trouble. We've got to go to him."

"Don't be silly, darling. You're imagining things. How could there be anyone here?"

I pushed back from him and looked up into his face. "There was, I tell you. There was! Up on the top."

Suddenly something caught my attention. A footprint. It was level with my eyes, a yard or so along a faintly defined path that led up steeply through the scrubby, tufty grass toward the top of the great crag. Clear and sharp in a small patch of soft snow, the imprint of a man's shoe!

"Brett, look!"

"What is it?"

But then some instinct warned me. A torrent of suspicions came swamping my mind. Disconnected things, connecting up. Terrors past and present merging into a single rushing stream. Springing from that footprint in the snow.

It was the mark of a rubber sole with a distinctive, deep-patterned tread. I had noticed it before, that same all-over design of triangles. Last night.

Brett's shoe!

Brett had been up there on top of the crag—from where I had heard a voice calling for help. A man's voice, muffled, but in *English!* Amazingly, that had not struck me as odd at the time.

Brett had expressed doubt that someone could be up there. Not *some*one—but Brett himself! He had been up there.

Other strange, unexplained incidents stabbed my brain. A fast-driven car, steered at me deliberately by some unknown driver in a dark, deserted back street of Palma; and Brett on the scene soon after. And in the Hôtel de l'Etoile in Nice yesterday morning, another car mysteriously blocking the hired Renault when we needed to get out quickly; and Brett not hurrying, refusing to abandon our car and find a taxi—that delay had caused us to miss Alexis. My mind winged back to London Airport—my handbag, containing my passport, snatched by someone I had thought at the time was just an ordinary sneak thief.

And now here. A cry for help which had made me press on along the path when I had been on the point of turning back. Suppose I had reached the viewpoint high above the valley, what then? A push from a hidden hand, a boulder crashing down? It wouldn't have taken much to send me hurtling to the rocks below.

My accident just now had been a mercy in disguise. A small fall had saved me from a worse one—a deadly one.

Could this man I had loved be my enemy? Why, why! I could only think of one possible explanation—that Brett was a Communist or a fellow traveler!

Only the Communists would wish Alexis to go on behaving as he was, destroying his reputation and alienating those who supported him. Only the Communists would want to stop me from reaching my uncle. And they were ruthless! To achieve a tactical advantage in their endless propaganda war, they would go to any lengths. Even murder meant nothing to them.

What did I really know about Brett Warrender? In our brief passionate love affair there had been so little time to explore ideas. So little time for me to get any hint of secret recesses in his mind.

Brett had been a rebel once—that was common knowledge. On leaving Cambridge, he had rejected the

idea of following Sir Ralph into the diplomatic service.
For two or three years he had knocked around the
world, on both sides of the Iron Curtain. Was it then
that he had been won over to the Communist ideology?
Had he, all the while since, been a "sleeper," slowly,
insidiously infiltrating himself, working into a position
where he would be of maximum use to the people he
served, whenever and wherever the occasion arose?
Awaiting his orders. Orders that he would obey with
blind dedication.

I backed away from Brett, staring up at him in
horror. Even now he might . . .

"What is it?" he asked, frowning. "Why are you
looking at me like that, Gail?"

With an immense effort, I took a grip on myself.
Brett mustn't see that I was afraid of him. I mustn't let
him guess. I said huskily, forcing out the words, "I'm
all right. Just a bit shaken up, that's all."

"It's not surprising." He reached out to me again,
but I evaded his arms.

I was suddenly seized by a violent fit of shivering.
"I'm cold," I muttered by way of explanation and
turned back toward the house. But I kept glancing
over my shoulder, scared to take my eyes off Brett.

"Careful, Gail!" he warned. "Watch where you're
going, or you'll fall again."

When we reached the track, it was wider and we
could walk two abreast. Brett said, "What was all that
about thinking you heard someone shout for help?"

I shrugged, somehow managing a nervous smile. "As
you said, I must have imagined it. The wind, I suppose."

He nodded. "The wind can play tricks in a wild
place like this. You ought not to have come out on
your own, you know."

And yet, last night, he had suggested that I should
do exactly that. To see the view!

Had it been Brett's plan to murder me all along,
right from the moment I'd announced that I was going
after Alexis? Was he still intending to kill me even
now, at any moment—quite openly and without any

pretense? In this wild place where he had contrived to bring me so cunningly, so calculatingly, it would be easy to make my death look like an accident.

But perhaps Brett might not kill me if he saw another way of keeping me from Alexis. At Nice he had merely delayed me; at London Airport he had tried to stop me from leaving the country by having my passport snatched.

Suppose . . . suppose now, even at this late hour, I pretended that I was taking his advice and giving up my quest for Alexis. If I told him I was going back home, would that save me?

I needed time to think. *Think!*

Back at the *mas,* I stood trembling and afraid while Brett raked the ashes and rebuilt the fire. After a moment, he turned to look up at me, an expression of concern on his face.

"Are you sure you're all right, Gail? Shall I make some coffee? That will help warm you up."

"Er . . . thanks."

I sat down on the couch where I had spent the night and held my coat open to the fire, trying to get warm, trying to shake off the feeling of panic that clogged my brain. Somehow, I had to get away from here.

When Brett came back from the kitchen and handed me a mug of coffee, I shrank away from him instinctively. But I mustn't let him see my revulsion. I mustn't let him guess that I suspected anything. I drove myself to respond to what he was saying—something about being sorry if he looked scruffy, but he had no razor with him. I said it didn't matter, that I must look just as scruffy myself.

"Would you like me to heat some water so you can have a decent wash?" he asked.

"Yes," I said vaguely. "No! I . . . I mean, I'll see to it myself, later."

He put down his mug on the thick wood beam that made a mantelshelf. His eyes caught and held my gaze.

"Gail . . . you're not regretting last night, are you?"

I shook my head and glanced away from him, down at the hearthrug. I couldn't take back those whispered words of love. Last night had been pure delight for me. I thought that I had found the truth again, but I'd been utterly wrong. Quite cynically, Brett had stirred the dormant love within me, just as I'd watched him stir the embers of the fire, making the flames leap high. Had it been just to satisfy his own casual desire, or to test his power over me? Or perhaps even—and I felt a flush of color stain my cheeks—because he thought I *expected* him to make love to me and wanted to keep me unsuspecting.

"Tell me you don't regret it, Gail," he insisted.

"No," I said quickly. "Of course I don't. But I feel a bit shaken up . . . from that fall."

His face relaxed, and he smiled at me. "You poor darling, it must have been worse than you made out. Is there anything I can get you?"

"No, nothing."

"Look, why not put your feet up and try to sleep a bit more. It's still quite early. Then when you wake up, I'll get some breakfast."

"All right."

I pulled a blanket around me and closed my eyes, pretending to settle down. But I kept rigidly alert, trying to gauge what Brett was doing as he moved about. I could sense him watching me, and I breathed deeply and steadily. After a while he seemed satisfied that I was asleep. He went over to the door, quietly letting himself out.

I jumped up and ran to the window, peering out from behind the curtain. I could see Brett walking with purposeful strides in the direction of the crag. I watched him until he disappeared from sight along the curving path. Had he gone to obliterate any telltale signs he might have left behind? To wipe out that incriminating footprint in the snow?

I remained standing at the window, staring out blindly. There were more snowflakes now, whirling past in the wind, beginning to settle on the Renault parked a

few yards away. Slowly, dimly, I became aware that
what I was looking at ought to have a special significance for me. Then at last, with a jolt, it penetrated
my fogged brain.

The car! Was that my chance of escape? My one
chance, while Brett was away from the house! I might
not get another.

Frantically, I tried to think, to remember. I knew
Brett hadn't bothered to lock the car, but had he left
the key in the ignition? I just had to pray he had.

I grabbed my handbag and was on my way to the
door when the shrill noise of the telephone pierced the
silence. For an instant I froze in panic, then I ran back
across the room to answer it. It could only be Dougal!

"Hello," I gasped breathlessly.

"Is that you, love?" The soft Highland lilt was unmistakable. "Er . . . can I speak to our mutual friend?"

I said urgently, "Please, Dougal, have you any news
of—?"

He interrupted me roughly. "No names! Yes, the
man in question has turned up again. He seems to be
mighty unsuccessful in keeping his whereabouts dark.
But what can he expect if he sticks to top resorts and
posh hotels?"

"Where is he?" I cried impatiently.

"Geneva, actually. But look, love, you'll have to be
careful. That's why I want to talk to . . . to you know
who. So be a good girl and put him on the phone."

"He's not here. He . . . he's gone out for a minute.
Can't you tell *me?*"

"I'll have to. I can't wait. I've got to get moving myself. Just explain that he must play it very canny if he
wants to keep your identity secret. Once the press boys
latch on to the fact that you're on the scene again, you
won't escape so easily a second time. Good luck, and
maybe I'll see you in Geneva."

"But where is . . . my uncle staying? Which hotel?"

"Didn't I say? It's the Cosmos, a damn great palace
of a place on the lakeside—west shore. You couldn't
miss it if you tried. Must be off."

I put down the phone, feeling a sudden uprush of hope. The call from Dougal coming at the precise moment that Brett was out of the way seemed like a good omen. Perhaps I would be able to escape from Brett, find Alexis, and get this terrible business finally sorted out.

All my hopes depended on a tiny key. The ignition key of the car.

Carefully, I opened the door and peered out. There was still no sign of Brett returning. Fear speeding me, I ran to the car and wrenched open the door. My heart skipped in relief. The key was there!

At the first attempt the engine merely kicked and grunted. I tried again, spinning it madly. It fired lumpily and died. But at the third feverish attempt the engine started and ran smoothly.

I had never driven a Renault before, but this was no time for caution, for feeling my way with the controls. As I swung onto the track, I glimpsed a movement in the mirror. Brett was running down from the crag, waving frantically for me to stop.

I put my foot down hard. The little car gagged, then responded. The track was rough, full of potholes and strewn with loose rocks. Taking it at speed, I was flung about in my seat as I clung grimly to the wheel, fighting to keep the car straight.

I flashed another glance in the mirror. Brett was falling back, the distance between us increasing fast. Then I was in among the pine trees, and he was lost from view.

Where the track joined the public road, I hesitated a moment, wondering which way to turn. But left, the way we had come, led back to the coast. I turned right, heading deeper into the mountains. Switzerland lay in that direction.

Chapter Twelve

The gun-metal sky had darkened almost to black, and it started to snow in earnest. I switched on the headlights, but they didn't seem to help much.

I had no time to spare for thinking, beyond the need to press on, somehow keeping the unfamiliar car on the narrow, tortuously twisting road. To escape from Brett.

After a few miles I came to a village, a small place that seemed completely shuttered against the snow. Suppose I were to stop and ask for protection—there might even be a local *gendarme*.

But protection against what? Against whom?

Against the man who had been my lover, who had become my lover again? The man who had been my companion on a journey of hundreds of miles, who had apparently done nothing but help and sustain me in my search for my uncle?

I passed straight through the village without stopping.

It seemed like hours before I reached a main highway, where there was other traffic to reassure me. But I had lost all sense of direction. A signpost by the roadside was obscured by driven snow, and I had to get out of the car and clean it with my fingers to read the directions. I found it was Routes Nationales 207. To Digne, it said. And Sisteron, Grenoble.

My geography was hazy, my mind hazier. I went back to the car and consulted the map Brett had bought, finding the road and tracing it with my finger. Digne was in the right direction, and Grenoble. A good road, it looked, right through to Geneva.

At Digne I stopped for gas and then pressed on again. I had never driven in such bad conditions. Even on the main highway I had to concentrate every second. Faster, bolder traffic passed me, flinging up a

veil of snow and slush that my windshield wipers
found difficult to clear.

The need to escape from Brett was not quite so
urgent now. Surely I was well clear of him. But through
all the confusion of my mind one thought stabbed re-
lentlessly. I had to reach Alexis. It seemed more vital
than ever before. Something told me that this was the
last opportunity I would be given. Fail now, and I
would have to abandon the search and return to Madeleine defeated.

It was past three in the afternoon when I reached
Grenoble. Daylight was fading fast and still the snow
fell, streaming back unendingly into the beams of my
headlights. My eyes pricked with the strain of peering
into blinding whiteness for hours on end; my head
throbbed. I longed to stop and rest. I needed a hot
drink, something to eat.

I decided to give myself a break of thirty minutes.

To avoid the problem of finding somewhere to park
in the center of the city, I waited until I was out on the
other side. Then I pulled up at the first roadside café I
came to. It turned out to be a drive-in for truck drivers,
a scruffy place. But I was past caring.

I found I was ravenous. I demolished a large plate
of veal cutlets and fried potatoes which was surpris-
ingly good. Then in the hot, steamy atmosphere, with
the pulsing beat of the jukebox, I could no longer fight
off tiredness. I dozed, my head resting against the bare
wall beside me. When I awoke, my coffee had gone
cold.

A truck driver at the next table got up and brought
me a fresh cup, flatly refusing to let me pay for it. I
realized that in my grubby coat and torn slacks I must
have looked in need of charity.

This act of kindness from a stranger gave me new
hope, and when I got outside I found the snow had
stopped. There was even a faint rose-red glow in the
western sky where the clouds were beginning to part.

Even so, the last lap to Geneva seemed a long one.
By the time I drew up at the customs post it had been

dark for some time. The Swiss officials dealt with me
efficiently, courteously. Within a few more minutes I
was entering the bright lights of Geneva.

A policeman, equally courteous and speaking excellent English, gave me directions to the Hotel Cosmos.
I drove past clanking streetcars and over a bridge, following the one-way system. There seemed to be hotels
everywhere, all along the waterfront. But then I spotted
the Cosmos—immense, a modern palace of white stone
and stainless steel and glass, bathed in a golden glow
from floodlights.

I turned into the driveway which ran the entire
width of the building and found an empty parking
space. I had the car door open when I hesitated.
Dougal's words came back to me in a rush. *Play it
canny . . . the press boys won't let you get away so
easily a second time.*

For all these long, tortuous miles, I'd been spurred
on by the need to reach Alexis. And now that I was
here, so close, I musn't ruin everything by being too
impetuous.

Yet I had to take risks if I was to get to see him.
And I was really past caring if the reporters *did* recognize me. I decided to walk straight into the hotel and
simply play it by ear.

Inside, the Cosmos was every bit as magnificent as
the hotel at Nice. But unlike the Edwardian splendor
of the Alpes-Maritimes, this was up-to-the-minute luxury—subdued, flattering lighting, acres of thick-pile
carpeting. Another place in the very top price bracket.

In the lobby there were a good many people around,
and I couldn't tell if any of them were reporters. Nobody took much notice of me. I got a few curious
stares as I walked in, but I put this down to my appearance. I cursed the torn slacks and grubby, crumpled coat. I should have thought to clean up a bit at the
café, but it was too late now.

The suave desk clerk looked down his nose at me.

"Que désirez-vous?"

"I wish to see Dr. Karel, please. I'll go straight up.

What is the number of his room?"

"Dr. Karel is seeing nobody," he said loftily and turned away from me.

"But it's very urgent. I'm his . . . his secretary." I held up my handbag. "I've brought some papers from England for him to sign."

"I hardly think that is likely, *m'selle.*"

For a moment I hesitated, wondering whether to make a scene. At a top-drawer place like this they would hate that. But I didn't want to draw attention to myself. Dejectedly, I turned away and started back across the spacious lobby. Maybe I could find a rear way to sneak in, bribe a porter, something like that.

There was a sudden flurry of commotion by the front entrance. The doorman, galvanized into action, leaped forward and held open the wide glass door, a service he'd not bestirred himself to perform for me.

Sweeping through, tall and poised, hips swaying, fully conscious of the heads that jerked to stare, came Belle Forsyth. She made a dramatic figure, supremely confident, her copper-red hair cascading to the shoulders of the black fur coat she wore.

She stopped dead when she saw me. We stood facing each other ten yards apart.

"You!" she gasped angrily. "What do you think you're doing here?"

I ran up to her in a rush. "Belle, I want to see Alexis. I've got to talk to him."

"It would be pointless," she said icily.

Two men had edged toward us, and made no secret of the fact that they were trying to listen. I guessed they were reporters.

"I *must* see him, Belle," I whispered. "It's important."

She made no effort to keep her voice down. "You are only making a fool of yourself, Gail. It ought to be obvious by now that your uncle has no wish to see you. Yet you persist in following us around."

"Please, Belle, can't we go somewhere private?" I said, glancing uneasily at the reporters. "Surely you understand . . . there are things I have a right to know."

"Right! What do you mean by *right?* You have no rights where Alexis is concerned, none at all. He is not even a relation, except by marriage. When your parents died, he very generously took you in, but you're old enough to fend for yourself now. Aren't you *ever* going to be satisfied?"

Dismayed, I faltered. "It . . . it's not for myself I'm asking, Belle. It's Madeleine."

"Madeleine!" she spat contemptuously. "That hysterical madwoman! Alexis has had enough of her. She's been like a millstone around his neck for years, and he's sick to death of it. Can't you understand, Gail, he's a flesh-and-blood male—and now at last he's got a chance to *live!* To enjoy the good things of life. If you're so concerned about your aunt, then it's up to you to look after her. I doubt if the Warrenders will turn her out of Deer's Leap. But if they do, Madeleine will just have to go into a mental home. That's where she really belongs."

I was speechless at her vicious outburst. As I groped for words, I saw the desk clerk hurrying over to intervene.

"I am so sorry, *madame,* if this . . . this young woman is annoying you. I have already informed her that Dr. Karel will see no one."

Belle shrugged carelessly. "She doesn't bother me. She can beg until she's blue in the face, but it won't make the slightest difference."

She didn't even glance at me again but turned her back and walked off with supreme contempt. She was heading for the elevator, but when I tried to follow her, the clerk blocked my path.

"You heard what *madame* said. I must ask you once again to leave the hotel."

In despair, I saw Belle step into one of the elevators; the doors closed upon her. Some instinct told me to watch the indicator. The needle swept right to the top, the ninth floor.

The two reporters huddled around me.

"Miss Fleming, why do you think your uncle refuses to see you?"

"How do you account for Dr. Karel's sudden change of viewpoint after all the years he's been . . . ?"

I shook my head at them, too choked with misery to speak. Out of the corner of my eye I saw the desk clerk signal to a porter, and I knew I was going to be thrown out. Glancing around desperately, I spotted the illuminated sign of the ladies' room. I turned and fled there.

Once inside the door, I stood breathlessly, undecided what to do. I knew that in a few moments they would send someone in to fetch me out. Two elegant, silver-haired women doing their faces before the pink-tinted mirror turned to stare at me.

I looked around wildly and noticed a small door tucked away in a corner. I guessed it must be for staff use. It represented my only hope, and I prayed it was unlocked.

It led me through to a narrow corridor, lit by unshaded bulbs. A few yards to the right was a service elevator with iron lattice gates and, alongside, stone stairs leading up and down. I heard a door slam somewhere behind me, then footsteps. I dived for the staircase and started to run up.

By the time I reached the third landing I was panting, and I paused to get my breath back. From below I heard the elevator gates slam, then a series of clicks and the whine of the cage ascending.

Was someone coming after me? I ran up a few more steps and pressed against the wall, so as not to be seen. The elevator stopped at the third floor and a girl got out, a chambermaid, carrying an armful of linen. As she passed the foot of the staircase she noticed me. Hastily, I pretended to be walking down. She looked at me a little strangely, I thought, but gave me a smiling nod and went on, disappearing through a swinging door.

The elevator stood invitingly open. I stepped inside, dragged the gates across and pressed the button with the figure 9.

On the top floor was a swinging door like the one

the maid had come through on the third floor. I carefully pushed it open a couple of inches and listened. There seemed to be no one around, so I slipped through.

I found myself in a circular hallway. Aside from the service door I had used and the guests' elevator, there were only two other doors. This was the top floor, so presumably these were penthouse suites. At least, having only two possibilities made my task easier.

My encounter in the lobby with Belle had only strengthened my resolve to see my uncle and plead with him to return home—for Madeleine's sake, for his own sake, for the sake of all those people who believed in him. And I had to warn Alexis about Brett and the Communists, make him understand that what he was doing could only bring satisfaction to his enemies.

But now there was an added motive driving me on—anger! Blind, stubborn anger. I refused to be brushed off by Belle, on his behalf, so casually and so contemptuously. Somehow, I was going to confront Alexis himself. I was determined to let him know my mind, even if, at the end, it achieved nothing.

I tossed a coin mentally and went to the door on the left. I knocked.

Would Alexis answer it himself? I prayed it wouldn't be Belle. But if so, I was ready to push my way in past her.

There was no answer, so I knocked again, loudly. The door was suddenly flung open, and I knew at once that I'd chosen wrongly. A short, pink-faced man stood there rocking unsteadily, a large glass in his hand. He leered at me.

"*Excusez-moi . . .*" I said. My limited French deserted me. "I was looking for Dr. Karel."

"*Ach so!*" he grunted, obviously not understanding. Breathing brandy fumes, he grabbed at my hand, trying to drag me inside.

Hastily, I pulled away from him. He glared at me with bloodshot eyes, muttered something, and slammed the door.

Scared that the hotel would be sending someone after me at any moment, I ran to the door of the other suite and rapped loudly.

A man's voice responded, *"Qui est là?"*

I had a sudden fear that if I said my name Alexis might refuse to let me in.

I called, *"C'est la femme de chambre, monsieur"* and hoped that the thickness of the door would mask my poor accent.

"Entrez."

My heart racing painfully, I opened the door and stepped inside.

It was a large, luxuriously appointed suite, softly lit by wall sconces and silk-shaded table lamps. Only one person was in there—Alexis. He lay comfortably stretched out on a long, gold brocade sofa, reading a newspaper. He had his back to me.

I closed the door quietly and stood waiting for him to turn around and see me. Seconds went past, each seeming like a minute. My palms were moist, and I could feel a pulse throbbing at my temple. I watched as, slowly, Alexis reached out to a glass ashtray on a low ebony-topped table and flicked ash from the cigar he was smoking.

At last, aware of my presence, my silence, Alexis closed his newspaper and swung around to look at me. But I saw no sign of pleased recognition in his eyes. Only a glint of anger.

"Qu'est-ce que vous voulez?" he asked irritably.

My throat felt so tight and constricted that I could only manage a whisper as I took a step toward him.

"Alexis!"

In a quick, startled movement he sprang to his feet and faced me. And in that same instant I knew the truth. It swept over me, engulfed me, drowned me.

This man was not Alexis Karel. He was not my uncle, but an impostor!

Chapter Thirteen

Standing by the lakeside, my fingers gripping the cold stone of the balustrade, I stared down into the dark water. A million reflected lights danced upon the surface, distorted to shivering needles by the blur of my tears.

Only minutes before I had been escorted down from the penthouse floor of the Cosmos and requested not to return. Warned not to set foot in the hotel again.

While, shocked and horrified, I stood staring at the man who looked so much like Alexis, he had fled without a word, retreating to an inner room. A moment later Belle Forsyth had emerged and started to hustle me outside.

"Why do you persist like this, Gail?" she demanded angrily. "I told you that your uncle will not see you."

I shook myself free of her.

"That man is not my uncle!" I shouted. "He isn't Alexis!"

I saw the swift startled narrowing of her eyes. Then, recovering quickly, Belle caught hold of me in a vicious grip, forcing me toward the door.

"What stupid nonsense you talk! I can't imagine what you hope to gain by it."

I grabbed at the door frame and clung to it frantically.

"What are you up to, Belle? What's it all about? What has happened to Alexis? Where is he?"

"Alexis is through there in the bedroom, of course. And he won't be coming out until you have gone. Just get this into your head once and for all—he doesn't want to see you. He doesn't want anything more to do with you, ever. Just stay out of his life, that's all he asks."

Across the circular hall, the elevator had stopped.

Two men stepped out. One was some sort of manager, sleek in a black jacket and pinstriped trousers; the other wore a porter's uniform.

Belle called, "Thank goodness you've come! I think she must be out of her mind."

As they advanced on me, I said desperately, "You don't understand—the man in there isn't Dr. Karel at all! He's an impostor."

They ignored my protests. I might not have spoken. The porter took over from Belle, holding my arm in a powerful, no-nonsense grip. The other man addressed me sternly, with only the thinnest veil of courtesy.

"I trust you will not make any further disturbance, *m'selle*. If you will please just leave the hotel quietly, we will say no more of this incident."

"Why won't you listen to me?" I shouted. "I tell you it isn't Dr. Karel in there."

They weren't prepared to waste time arguing with me. I was torn roughly from my hold on the door frame and bustled to the elevator. Not the lift that waited with its doors yawning open—that way I might be seen by hotel guests. I was taken through the swinging door to the service elevator.

The clerk or assistant manager or whoever he was didn't even bother to come down with us; presumably he was returning to the suite to make apologies to Belle. It was clear that the porter, a burly six-foot-plus type, would have no difficulty handling me on his own.

On the ground floor he led me to the nearest exit, next to the kitchens.

"Please, *m'selle,* do not try to cause more trouble." Then with a fleeting little smile, as if to show there was nothing personal in it, he pushed me outside and slammed the door in my face.

An aching numbness inside me, I stumbled around the huge hotel with some vague idea of making another attack through the front entrance. But as I went up the steps, the doorman spotted me at once and came forward meaningfully. Defeated, I gave up and crossed the wide roadway to the lakeside.

All other thoughts were forced from my mind as the frantic question pounded: What had happened to Alexis? Where was he?

The answer came swiftly, with no shred of doubt to offer me comfort. My uncle must be dead. *Murdered!*

With sickening clarity, I knew that I had uncovered a most sinister plot. An elaborate, meticulously worked-out plot to discredit Alexis Karel and everything he stood for.

For the Communists, it was not good enough simply to remove Alexis from the scene—to kidnap him, or arrange to have him killed. Any such plan would defeat their objective. Alexis Karel, on his disappearance or death, would spring into the headlines of the world's press as a noble martyr, an inspiring symbol of resistance to oppression.

So instead they had devised a scheme to substitute a false Alexis. An Alexis Karel whose callous betrayal of his sick wife and vulgar flaunting of a young mistress in some of the flashiest hotels in Europe was so outrageous that it would shock the millions of people who had revered him—from personal friends like Sir Ralph Warrender to the ordinary man and woman on both sides of the Iron Curtain.

The deception had been so clever—the fake Alexis made to look so incredibly like the real one—that it would fool almost everybody. Only someone who knew Alexis intimately would be able to tell the difference. Only someone like me!

Convinced that I was right, I still felt dazed at the amount of planning that must have been required, the painstaking details of organization and timing. And I guessed that the Communists had taken into their calculations the fact that Alexis Karel's niece, Gail Fleming, the person closest to him apart from his wife, would be conveniently out of the way in the United States.

My sudden return home, my decision to track down and confront my uncle must have jeopardized the whole operation. I had to be stopped. At all costs I had to be prevented from exposing the truth.

But killing me would be dangerous, causing questions to be asked, suspicions aroused—unless my death could appear beyond doubt to be accidental. There must not be the faintest breath of a hint that I might have been murdered.

And so Brett had been picked for the job. Brett Warrender, well-known TV personality, close family friend and at one time my lover. An incredible but unimpeachable choice!

I leaned against the stone balustrade and wept. Tears of grief and pity—for Alexis, for Madeleine, for myself. Tears of fear and bitter anger.

Since my "accident" at the *mas,* I had understood Brett's true role, known that his orders were to prevent me from reaching Alexis—even if it meant killing me. But I had believed that the Communists were merely taking advantage of circumstance—seeing Alexis Karel's sudden desertion of his wife for a younger woman (and consequent damage to his prestige) as a useful piece of propaganda for their cause.

The truth was far more terrible.

"Gail, I've been looking for you!"

Even as I turned, recognizing the voice, Dougal's arm came around my shoulder. His finger tilted up my chin so that our eyes met.

"You're crying," he said. "And no wonder! I've just heard about the scene you had with Belle Forsyth."

"Oh, Dougal!"

With a sob of relief, I clutched at the lapels of his tweed overcoat. He was my only friend in this hostile city.

He held me for a moment and then said, "You're shivering. Are you cold?"

I shook my head, unable to speak.

He said sympathetically, "It must have been hell for you. Actually, I had another interview with your uncle when I arrived this afternoon—I came up by plane. It surprised me how ready he still is to talk, considering he's been trying like mad to dodge the press. Naturally I don't agree with his I'm-all-right-Jack philosophy, but coming from a man like him it makes damn good copy." Dougal hesitated. "Gail, I didn't mention you were on your way to see him. I thought you wouldn't want me to. But I wish I had now. I might have been able to warn you of the reception you were likely to get. Just a while ago, I went back to the Cosmos to see if you and Brett had turned up—where is he, incidentally?—and the press chaps were talking about the way that Forsyth bitch had lammed into you. If you want my opinion, your uncle is a bastard!"

"He isn't my uncle!" I burst out, suddenly finding my voice.

Dougal stared at me. "You mean you're not Alexis Karel's niece? But Brett said—"

"No, no! I mean that the man in the hotel isn't Alexis Karel at all. He's a fake. I've seen him. Just now I went up there . . . in a service elevator . . . and I managed to get into their penthouse. It's *not* my uncle!"

"Now hold on a minute, Gail! You say you actually saw this man, you talked to him, and he isn't Alexis Karel?"

"That's right! But I didn't talk to him—I didn't get a chance. As soon as he saw me, he looked scared to death and rushed into the bedroom. And then Belle came out, and the next minute a manager type and a porter came up to fetch me. They wouldn't listen to a word I said, Dougal. I was taken down in the service elevator again and thrown out with a warning not to go back there."

"Gail," he broke in reproachfully, "what you're really saying is that your uncle wouldn't talk to you. I don't blame you for being upset. It was a wretched thing to have happened. But that's no reason for making wild accusations about him being a phony."

"But don't you see," I insisted, "this explains everything! It's all a horrible plot to destroy Alexis—to destroy his good name, I mean, and make everyone turn against him—just when his book is coming out with all those terrible revelations about the Communists. You realize what they've done? They've *murdered* Alexis and put this other man in his place. It's a good enough likeness to deceive most people, but I know my uncle too well to be taken in. That's why they dared not let me catch up with this fake Alexis Karel. That's why he and Belle keep moving from one place to another."

"Gail!" said Dougal uneasily. "I honestly don't think..."

I rushed on, sure I could make him understand. "Brett is mixed up in it too, Dougal. He pretended to be helping me find Alexis, but all the time he was really making sure that I didn't succeed."

"For God's sake!" Dougal protested. "You must be out of your mind suggesting that Brett is mixed up with the Commies! It's a fantastic idea."

"Is it? Then why did he try to kill me?"

Dougal stared at me, his mouth gaping. "*Brett* tried to *kill* you?"

"Yes, twice! The first time was in Palma when a car nearly ran me down in some back street—I'm sure it was him. And this morning, at the little *mas* he took me to up in the mountains, he tried to make me fall over a cliff. Of course, he made it seem like an accident. But there wasn't anyone else within miles, and anyway I saw his footprint in the snow. So as soon as I got a chance, when Brett had gone out—that was when you phoned, Dougal—I took the car and drove off. Brett came chasing after me, trying to stop me, but luckily I was able to get away from him."

Dismayed, I realized Dougal was by now not even listening. He was refusing to believe a single word I was saying. He evaded my eyes, and I could sense the sudden withdrawal of his sympathy.

"I'm sorry, Gail, but it's really going too far—trying to drag Brett in like that. I realize these past few days have been a terrible strain on you, and in a way I can understand you inventing this story about a fake Alexis Karel, but—"

"I didn't invent it! I tell you the man I saw wasn't my uncle."

"How can you be so certain? A quick glimpse of

somebody whose one and only idea was to get away from you, because he felt so ashamed!"

"He wasn't ashamed—he was *scared*. He knew that if he stayed in the room, I'd see through him. He knew he couldn't hope to fool me."

Dougal was silent for a minute, thoughtful. "You say that the Communists have hatched up an elaborate plot to smash Alexis Karel's reputation and destroy the value of his book. But don't you see, Gail, it could just as easily be the other way around. That *you* are desperately trying to prevent your uncle from toppling off his pedestal, by inventing this whole story of a Communist plot. Try and ask yourself—if you were on the outside, looking in, which version would you believe?"

"Which do *you* believe, Dougal?" I whispered. "Me or the Communists?"

Swiftly, his hand closed over mine. He said gently, "You're confused, Gail. All mixed up. I'm sorry to sound unsympathetic. Maybe you really do believe all this about a phony Alexis Karel, maybe you've convinced yourself—I don't know. But you mustn't try and drag Brett Warrender into it. That really isn't fair!"

"I tell you, Brett tried to kill me!"

He gave an exasperated sigh. "If you persist in saying that, Gail, you can't expect me to help you."

I jumped on his words eagerly. *"Will* you help me, Dougal?"

"If I can," he said cautiously, "of course I will."

"Then send this story back to your paper. Not about Brett, if you don't want to—but all the rest of it. You'll have it exclusive, remember—that's what you wanted, isn't it? And when the *Globe* has published it, other papers will pick it up."

"Oh yes, they'd do that, all right! They'd make the *Globe* a laughingstock. No newspaper would risk its neck on such stuff. There's not a shred of evidence."

"But it's *true!*" I flashed back bitterly. "I give you my word it's true."

"You're an interested party, Gail. So I'm afraid your

word wouldn't carry much weight. In fact, quite the
reverse. Believe me, there isn't an editor in Fleet Street
who would touch it."

It was as if there was a barrier between us, a solid
wall that blocked off understanding. In my innocence
I'd thought I had only to tell what I knew about the
impostor who called himself Alexis Karel, and I would
immediately be believed. But now I knew differently.

"Oh, Dougal, what am I going to do?" I cried in
despair.

I might have guessed what his advice would be.

"If I were you, Gail, I'd go back to England. Back
home."

"But how can I? How can I with that man still acting a part, and Alexis—dead? I can't allow them to
win without fighting back."

Dougal let out a long breath, as if regretting his own
weakness in pandering to me.

"If you like, if it will help reconcile you, Gail, I'll
go and have another talk with Dr. Karel. I can pretend
there are one or two points I want clarified from my
interview this afternoon. With any luck, I might even
get hold of him right now."

"Oh, would you really, Dougal!" I was ready to
clutch at any straw. "If you could talk to him, knowing
what I've told you, you might catch him out. He might
easily slip up and give himself away."

Dougal shook his head. "I shan't be trying to catch
him out, Gail, for the simple reason that I believe he
really is the man he claims to be. But I'd hate you to
think I'm not willing to help when you're in trouble.
If Brett were here, I could leave him to worry about
you. But God knows where he is at this moment. Quite
possibly he never even got away from that place you
were staying at. There've been reports of heavy snow-
falls in the Basses Alpes. I reckon you must have been
lucky and got out of the district just in time."

If Brett was stuck at La Retraite, then I didn't have
any cause to fear him. Not for the moment. At least
it gave me time to act—while he couldn't interfere.

Dougal said, "Look, Gail, I don't like leaving you standing around here while I'm gone. Suppose I take you along to the next hotel, and you can wait for me in the bar."

I shook my head. "No, I feel such a mess. I'll sit in the car. It's parked outside the Cosmos."

Dougal walked over the road with me to the Renault.

"I'll try not to be too long," he said. "You stay here, promise!" He paused, looking at me intently. "You've done some foolish things this last day or two, Gail. But the stupidest by far was running away from Brett. Now don't run away again."

I watched Dougal's tall figure heading for the entrance of the Hotel Cosmos. Despite his quick strides, he seemed to move reluctantly. I knew I ought to feel grateful to him; he had tried to be kind. Yet I felt a bitter hostility because he refused to accept my word.

But, I argued, he must have *some* doubt in his mind to have agreed to go and see the man who claimed to be Alexis. And Dougal was shrewd—I was certain of that. Forewarned with what I'd told him, surely he would find some chink in the impostor's armor. It would need only a few careful probing questions, and Dougal would be convinced that I was right.

I settled to wait, trying to hold off the thousand agonizing thoughts that bombarded my mind. At this moment, my own personal danger seemed to be the least of my worries. Most of all, I was concerned about Madeleine. I knew now, I was quite *certain,* that Alexis was dead—and it would be my dreadful task to break it to my aunt. The news would shatter her.

Dougal was back in less than ten minutes, startling me as he opened the car door. He slid into the seat beside me, without speaking.

"What . . . what happened?" I asked faintly, fearfully.

Dougal hesitated. When he spoke his voice was harsh.

"He wasn't there, and he won't be back. It's getting

to be a habit with that man—he's skipped again. Checked out of the hotel with Belle Forsyth, and nobody's got a clue where they're heading."

Chapter Fourteen

I was flying back home, defeated.

But what else could I do? I had lost my luggage way back in Nice and had only the grubby, torn clothes I had on. And very little money left.

In any case, what was the point of staying on in Geneva? The man who pretended to be Alexis had vanished again, and this time—I knew it instinctively —he had vanished for good. His job was done now. A painstakingly thorough job of character assassination. The Communists would not risk another appearance, when his genuineness might be challenged.

And what of the actual physical assassination, my poor uncle's murder? Who had done that job?

Was it Belle Forsyth, who I had liked and trusted, whose coming to Deer's Leap had seemed to us all such a blessing? She had been right there on the spot.

Or could it have been Brett? I shuddered violently, trying to close my mind to the horrifying possibility.

When the plane landed at London Airport, it was nearly midnight. A rainswept February night, cold and desolate. I had difficulty in getting a taxi to take me all the way to Deer's Leap and had to offer the driver a handsome bonus as an inducement.

He was a fat, cheerful Cockney who expected to pass the journey in chitchatty conversation. But he soon realized that I was a dead loss and lapsed into offended silence.

I sat hunched in the rear seat, my brain battered to a daze.

I owed a lot to Dougal Fraser. He had been very kind, yet I knew he was relieved to put me on a plane, to put me out of his mind. I'd not had enough money left to pay my fare to London, and the return ticket from Palma was useless. Dougal had seen to everything, using his credit card and saying we could sort it all out later. And he'd promised to have the Renault returned to the car-rental firm.

"Don't worry about any of it, Gail. Just go home and forget all this."

Forget! I would never forget.

It was a living nightmare. Somehow—however long it took me—I would force the truth out into the open. Nothing could bring my uncle back to life, but the name Alexis Karel must be restored in people's minds as a symbol of integrity and hope.

And yet I had no idea how I was going to do this. The Communists had planned it all meticulously, leaving no weaknesses, no cracks for me to probe.

It seemed to me I would have to start at Deer's Leap. That was where it had all begun. Belle had been installed there long in advance, cunningly working herself into the household, ready for the ghastly plan to be put into operation. So it was at Deer's Leap I must start searching for evidence.

At least I would be with Madeleine. My poor aunt! There was no getting out of it now; she would have to be told *something*. But what I didn't know.

At Deer's Leap, too, I could share my dreadful knowledge with Rudi. He would help me.

I couldn't make up my mind how much I was going to tell Sir Ralph. In some ways—terrible as the new situation was—it must come as a relief to him. It would give him back his lost faith in Alexis, and he would become my ally in trying to expose the truth.

But, inevitably, telling Sir Ralph would mean revealing the part Brett had played, and I dreaded having to do that. Brett was his only son, the son he was so proud of. To learn of Brett's involvement would break Sir Ralph's heart.

The time ahead was dark with uncertainty, as black and impenetrable as the night that surrounded me. The car sped on through lashing rain, the windshield wipers and the driver's wheezy breathing a monotonous background to my tortured thoughts.

Deer's Leap was in darkness, not a light showing anywhere. I hadn't enough cash to pay off the driver and had to ask him to wait while I woke Rudi.

I pulled the old-fashioned bell handle. Nothing happened, and I pulled it again, forcefully, the jangle echoing loudly in the night silence.

At last a light went on upstairs, sending a feeble glow down into the hall. Then the hall lights themselves came on. I heard the heavy bolts drawn back. The front door opened a few inches, on the chain, and a pale face appeared at the slit.

"Who's there?"

Freda Aiken! I could have done without her at the moment.

"It's Gail Fleming. I'm sorry to have got you up, Miss Aiken, but I haven't a key with me."

"Oh!"

The door was shut again and the chain freed. Then Freda opened up for me. She was wearing a blue woolen dressing gown, and her hair was in curlers.

"Nobody told me you were coming back tonight, Miss Fleming," she said in an aggrieved tone.

"I didn't know myself until a few hours ago. I'm sorry to have disturbed you. I was hoping it would be Mr. Bruckner, but I know he's rather a heavy sleeper. I'll have to go up and wake him, because I haven't enough cash with me for the taxi. But there's no need for you to wait up, thank you, Miss Aiken. You should get straight back to bed."

I invited the driver to come inside and wait. As I hurried upstairs, Freda Aiken remained there with him in the hall, as if she thought he couldn't be trusted.

Rudi was right about being a heavy sleeper. I had to go into his room and actually shake him before at last he muttered drowsily and opened his eyes. He gave a short, startled gasp and sat bolt upright.

"Gail! What are you doing here? What's happened?"

"It's a long story, Rudi. I'll tell you in a minute, but first will you please give me four pounds so I can settle up with the taxi driver. I've come straight from the airport."

"Yes, of course. My wallet is over there on the chest of drawers. Help yourself." He threw back the blankets and slid out of bed, dragging a short paisley robe over his white pajamas. "I've been worried out of my mind, Gail—not hearing from you for two days. Is everything all right?"

"Oh, Rudi, far from it! Come downstairs, and I'll tell you."

Four pound notes in my hand, I went on ahead of him to pay off the driver. Freda Aiken was still there, having a murmured conversation with the man, no doubt pumping him. But there wasn't anything he could tell her beyond the fact, possibly, that I had come off the Geneva plane.

Rudi had come downstairs by the time I'd seen the driver out. He took hold of my arm, urging me toward the Oak Room.

Once again, I apologized to Freda Aiken. "I'm sorry to have disturbed you, but I'm afraid I couldn't help it.'

She nodded, her face quite blank. But she astonished me by saying suddenly, "I'll make some tea."

"Thanks, but there's no need," said Rudi hastily.

"But why not, Mr. Bruckner? I expect we could all do with a cup. I know I could."

I was in an agony to get rid of the woman. If she'd felt an iota of genuine concern, I wouldn't have minded, but I was sure it was pure nosiness on her part. I said rather shortly, "You go ahead and make tea for yourself if you want to. But not for us, thanks. Good night!"

With that I walked into the Oak Room. Rudi followed me in and firmly shut the door.

"Gail, for heaven's sake, what's happened?"

I shook my head warningly. "Keep your voice down. I expect she's trying to listen, and I don't want her to know about it—not for the present, anyhow."

I sank into one of the leather armchairs while Rudi

stood over me, looking down at me anxiously.

"Oh, Rudi—it's terrible! The man with Belle isn't Alexis at all. He's an impostor!"

Rudi gave a startled, unbelieving gasp.

"I finally caught up with them at a hotel in Geneva. Belle tried to keep me away from him, but I managed to get to their suite. And when he looked at me, I knew at once. Before I could speak to him, though, he ran into another room, and then Belle appeared and I was thrown out. The man's a fake, Rudi. He's been made to look exactly like Alexis, but I know he's a fake!"

All the color had drained from Rudi's face, leaving an ashen mask. "What does this mean? What's happened to Alexis?"

I stared up at him, willing him to tell me I was utterly wrong in what I believed. Yet I was certain that he couldn't.

"You know the Communists even better than I do, Rudi. You know the ruthless way they plan and scheme. If they wanted to destroy Alexis Karel, to destroy everything he stood for, to make his very name hated and despised, isn't this just the sort of thing they're capable of?"

Rudi was standing with his eyes closed, swaying slightly as if he felt faint. When he opened his eyes again, I saw the shock and grief in them.

"They've killed him!" he whispered in a long anguished breath. "They've murdered him!"

For endless silent seconds we stared at each other while our minds took in the full horror. Not just that Alexis was dead, but the terrible implications of his murder, the ruthlessness we were up against. I had already faced it before, this moment of appalled realization. But now, with Rudi, I experienced it again, no less intensely than the first time.

I said at last, "The Communists tried everything to stop me catching up with that pair. They knew I wouldn't be deceived, any more than you would be, Rudi. They even tried to kill me—twice they tried." I hesitated, taking a deep breath. "And there's something else. Brett is involved in it, too. That's why he insisted on coming with me. It was his job to keep tabs on me and make sure I didn't ever get near Belle and that man." My voice cracked. "It . . . it was Brett who tried to kill me."

"*Brett!* You don't know what you're saying, Gail!"

He held out his arms to me, as if pleading with me to stop telling him these terrible things. I rose to my feet, clutching at him in a desperate need for reassurance. His hand touched my hair gently.

"Not *Brett*, Gail! These other things, they may be true—I don't know what to think. But Brett Warrender, no! I haven't liked him, but only because of the way he hurt you. I can't believe he was involved in anything like that."

"He *is*, I tell you! I ought to have been suspicious of him from the start. I ought to have guessed he was up to something when he was so determined to stick with me."

"Perhaps," said Rudi hesitantly, "it was as I suggested before—that Brett still loves you."

That was exactly what Brett had wanted me to believe, I thought with a stabbing remembrance. He had wanted to lull any possible doubts I might have had about him. That night we spent together in the little *mas,* deep in the mountains of Provence. In my fierce joy, I imagined that our love was being reborn. Afterward, in the gray light of morning, I'd concluded sadly that to Brett it had been just an interlude.

But it had taken an attempt to murder me before I saw Brett's lovemaking as the coldly calculating piece of seduction it really was.

"Rudi, what am I to do?" I cried desperately. "How can I expose this plot? How can I *prove* it?"

Rudi didn't answer. In the silence I heard a sudden flurry of raindrops lash the leaded window panes.

"Somehow," I went on with agonized determination, "somehow or other we've got to find evidence. We've got to show that Belle Forsyth is a Communist and was deliberately planted here at Deer's Leap. And we've got to find some way of proving that the Communists murdered Alexis."

Rudi interrupted me. "Gail . . . can you really be so sure that Alexis is dead?"

"Of course he's dead—you said so yourself! Otherwise, there would always be a risk of the whole story coming out."

"No, I meant . . . can you really be quite positive it wasn't Alexis you saw in Geneva? You could have made a mistake."

I shook my head emphatically. "I wasn't mistaken, Rudi. I *know* I wasn't. I came face to face with the man, hardly six feet away, and it was definitely not Alexis."

"What exactly makes you so certain?"

"Everything! It's difficult to pin it down, but when you know a person as I knew Alexis, you can't be deceived."

"But you say you only saw him for a few seconds, and you didn't get a chance to speak to him. Just consider . . . if in fact Alexis *has* run off with Belle Forsyth, abandoning poor Madeleine, then he'll be feeling terribly guilty. When he was suddenly confronted by you, Gail, he'd have been deeply ashamed. That would be enough to make him act differently—oddly."

I took a step back, out of Rudi's arms, gripped by a sense of cold betrayal.

"You too!" I murmured bitterly. "You think I'm imagining it all, don't you, because I can't accept the truth? Oh, Rudi, do you honestly believe I would wish Alexis dead in *any* circumstances?"

He shook his head in a bewildered, unhappy way. His voice was thick with emotion. "I don't know. Perhaps it's because I can't bear to believe that he's dead, Gail. Not in the way you suggest. Not murdered! If that were really true, then I think . . . I think I should want to die myself. I keep remembering that night he disappeared—going over and over it in my mind."

I felt a sudden flood of pity for him. "But, Rudi, you can't blame yourself for what happened."

He turned away and started to fiddle nervously with the spiraled cord of the telephone on the library desk. The movement jogged the phone in its cradle, making the bell give a sharp ting.

"Gail, there is something I haven't told you. Something you ought to know. It rather alters things."

"What is it, Rudi? Tell me."

I watched him struggling to overcome his reluctance. Then he squared his shoulders, and his eyes met mine.

"Alexis *was* having an affair with Belle Forsyth. Here at Deer's Leap. I know that for a fact, Gail. It had been going on for about three months."

Hands pressed to my throat, I stared at Rudi. I was too choked to speak.

"I didn't tell you before," he said. "I knew how it would upset you. But that was why, when the news came through about them turning up together in Majorca, I was forced to accept it. I knew that Alexis had deserted Madeleine for Belle." Rudi sighed deeply. "You can imagine how wretched I've felt these last few months, knowing what was going on between them —right here under the same roof as poor Madeleine. But what could I do? I swear I never dreamed it would come to this, otherwise I'd have written and told you. If only I had. You might have been able to appeal to your uncle before things went too far."

I felt sick with misery. Now, just as my faith in Alexis seemed to have been given back to me, it was being snatched away again with this horrible revelation. How could my uncle have carried on in such a heartless way? Any other man, perhaps, but not Alexis Karel! I thought of the pact between us in my childhood, a pact which had never needed putting into words. That at all costs Madeleine must be sheltered and protected, never again allowed to suffer as she had suffered in the past. I had lived by that principle ever since. How could it possibly have meant so little to Alexis?

"It's not true, Rudi!" I said stubbornly. "I don't believe it."

"I'm afraid there's no doubt, Gail. They were careful, but they couldn't conceal it from me completely. I saw her slipping out of his bedroom on more than one occasion in the early hours."

I crossed to the fireplace and stood there leaning my forehead against the smooth stone mantel. However much I wanted to disbelieve this, I couldn't. I knew Rudi was speaking the truth.

He said earnestly, "Gail, the man you saw in that hotel in Geneva . . . I believe it *was* Alexis. I think it must have been."

I had been so completely sure, so *certain*. Yet . . .

Numbly, I tried to recall the scene, down to the last fragment of detail. Clouded at first, unfocused, the picture in my mind slowly cleared.

The large penthouse suite, luxuriously furnished, softly lit. The man stretched comfortably on a gold brocade sofa, reading a newspaper, his back turned to me. At that moment I hadn't doubted he was Alexis.

Then, irritated by my silent presence, the man had turned to look at me. He had said sharply, *"Qu'est-ce que vous voulez?"*

While this was happening, and now in my recollection, it was still Alexis. At which precise moment had I known, with a rush of certainty, that the man was not my uncle?

I had whispered his name. Startled, he had sprung to his feet and spun around to face me. Yes, that was the moment!

I concentrated upon it, holding the image there. What was it that had told me this was not Alexis? The abundant white hair, the strong straight nose, the whole shape of his head, the upright posture, the square set of his shoulders—everything was right.

Except the eyes!

Eyes that didn't know me. Eyes that showed a sudden swift fear. They were not my uncle's eyes.

Or were they his? With an expression I had never seen in them before—*shame!* Was Rudi right?

I was in a panic now because my certainty was

shaken. Which was the truth? Which did I *want* to be the truth?

That Alexis was dead—murdered? That there was a ruthless Communist plot to destroy his name?

Or that Alexis was alive and well, having deserted Madeleine, rejected me, and thrown away all the ideals he had ever stood for?

I couldn't give an answer, even to myself.

I felt Rudi's hand on my shoulder. He spoke softly, gently. "Gail . . . dear Gail—you must be exhausted. Go to bed, and I'll bring you up something. You need to rest, to get some sleep."

Still leaning against the mantel, I stared down between my arms at the empty hearth. Unwanted to my mind there suddenly came the memory of the hearth at that little *mas* in the mountains, a massive rough-hewn slab of stone piled high with blazing pine logs.

At that moment, I couldn't imagine how I would ever sleep again.

Chapter Fifteen

As I crossed the room on my way up to bed, a sudden commotion just outside the door halted me. A clash of voices. Freda Aiken's, kept low, muttering persuasively, followed by Madeleine's, her high-pitched protest clearly audible through the solid oak panels.

"How dare you try and stop me! My husband has come home, and I want to see him."

For a fleeting second Rudi and I stared at each other in dismay before the door was abruptly flung open and my aunt burst in. She was wearing her quilted pink satin robe over her nightdress.

Seeing me there, Madeleine stopped in surprise, frowning. Then she broke into a warm smile of welcome.

"Gail, darling, so *you* are back as well!" She looked

anxiously from one to the other of us. "Where is he? Where is Alexis?"

My heart plunged. I was totally unprepared to face Madeleine tonight.

"I heard the car arrive," she was saying eagerly. "Quite a long while ago. I've been waiting and waiting for him to come up to me. In the end I couldn't bear to wait any longer, so I came down. Where is he?"

I went to her, leading her gently to one of the leather armchairs.

"Darling, it wasn't Alexis you heard arriving. It was me. I'm sorry, but Alexis isn't here—as you can see."

Her look of happy expectancy was wiped away. Her face crumpled, and she sank weakly into the chair.

"But I was so sure it was Alexis! Where is he? It's been such a long time now, and not a word from him."

From the doorway, Freda Aiken said, "Mrs. Karel ought to go straight back upstairs. In her state of health it's not right to jump out of a warm bed in the middle of the night. I can't be held responsible."

I knew the woman was right. But did she have to be quite so brutally direct and unsympathetic? I shook my head at her, warning her not to say any more.

"Madeleine, you really had better go back to bed. I'll come up with you."

In such an excited mood as this my aunt could behave exactly like a child—one moment easy to handle, the next obstinate and self-willed. Tonight, fortunately, she allowed herself to be persuaded.

She stood up again as I took her arm, and we walked slowly out of the room and across the hall. At the foot of the staircase, she paused, as if gathering her strength. Mounting one stair at a time, she held her free hand against her heart.

"I was so happy, Gail. I thought . . . I thought . . ."

"Don't try to talk now, darling. Get back to bed first."

Her acute disappointment, added to the labor of climbing the stairs, was making her very breathless. I made her stop for a few moments before we continued on up.

On the landing, Freda Aiken bustled past us, going ahead to straighten the bed. Madeleine turned to me, saying in a breathy whisper, "That woman isn't a bit like Belle. Dear Belle! I miss her, too—so much! I hope her friend will soon be better so that my Belle can come back to me."

I squeezed my aunt's thin arm in silent sympathy. What could I say to comfort her? Only empty lies that would have to be unsaid tomorrow. Tomorrow, I reminded myself firmly, Madeleine would have to be told. I had just a few hours left for reflection, before coming to a decision about what I was going to tell her.

In the bedroom, I waved Freda Aiken aside. Madeleine needed the most loving care just now—not efficient, impersonal nursing. I helped her into bed, smoothing the pillow and gently tucking her in.

In an undertone, I said to Freda, "Could she have another sleeping pill, do you think? Otherwise, I'm afraid she'll lie awake fretting."

"I suppose so," she said ungraciously. "I'd better go down and warm a drop of milk for her to have with it."

Madeleine smiled at me wanly. In the soft light of the bedside lamp, her golden eyes were huge and luminous. I saw in their depths the indelible mark of suffering, of sadness, of tragedy. My heart twisted in pity for her, thinking of what she yet had to face.

"I suppose it was silly of me, being so sure it was Alexis come home," she said. "But I was so hoping. Why has he been away so long, Gail, and not a letter —not even a telephone call? It isn't like Alexis, is it, to be thoughtless? I can't help being worried that something may have happened to him."

I ought to have told her then. I ought to have been honest with her. But I was too cowardly.

"There are all sorts of possible explanations, darling," I murmured weakly. My aunt was so innocently trusting that I felt stabbed through with guilt.

"I expect you're right, Gail dear. I'm just a silly woman with not enough to occupy my mind."

QUEST FOR ALEXIS

When Freda brought in the glass of warm milk,
Madeleine sat up to drink it, accepting without question the extra sleeping pill. She awarded the nurse a
faint smile.

"You do your best for me, don't you, Freda? And I
expect I can be a trial sometimes."

Freda Aiken set her lips, making no reply.

I kissed my aunt's pale forehead and left her with a
promise to come and see her first thing in the morning.

"Then we'll have a lovely long talk, won't we?" she
said eagerly. "It's so good to have you home, dear."

Rudi was waiting for me outside the door.

"You didn't say anything to her, Gail?"

I shook my head. "I couldn't, not tonight."

"No, of course not. Look, you go straight to bed
now, and I'll bring something to your room. A sandwich."

"No, Rudi—I couldn't eat."

"Well, just a cup of Ovaltine, then. You must have
something."

"I suppose so. Thanks."

Ten minutes later, when he knocked at my door, I
was already in bed and almost asleep. Rudi put the
beaker on the bedside table and sat down on the edge
of the bed.

I found I couldn't focus properly on his face. I felt
dizzy, and the bed seemed to be swaying and dipping
under me. It was as if I was drunk, or drugged, as if *I*
had taken the sleeping pill, not Madeleine. But I knew
it was the effect of exhaustion. Too much had happened to me in this one day.

Twenty-four hours ago I had been sleeping on a
couch in a primitive Provençal *mas,* with Brett beside
me on the hearthrug, rolled up in blankets. I had wakened in a gloriously happy mood, trusting him completely.

My trust had been so short-lived.

I could feel my brain working turgidly, like a ma-
chine that was filled with too thick oil.

Alexis dead. Brett a murderer. An almost perfect

double of my uncle, acting out an evil charade to destroy the value of his life's work.

Or was I wrong? Was Rudi right? I hated myself for feeling even the faintest stirring of doubt. Alexis and Belle, here at Deer's Leap—I could not dismiss that. Rudi had stood by and watched unhappily as the situation developed between them. But Alexis, I was still unalterably convinced, would never have deserted Madeleine so callously.

Which did I believe? Which did I *want* to believe?

"Oh, Rudi, what am I to do?"

He leaned forward and touched my forehead with his lips. "You poor darling, you're worn out. Here, drink this up and get to sleep."

Rudi held the beaker for me while I drank from it, as if I were a sick child. Then, as I lay back upon the pillows, he stood gazing down at me.

"If only things could have been different, Gail," he murmured. "I wish to God!"

I don't remember whether he finished the sentence. I couldn't keep my eyes open a moment longer. I slept deeply, and my dreams were a twisted, tangled nightmare of fear.

In the morning the sun was shining, filtering through the yellow curtains, filling my bedroom with a warm golden light.

But I lay cold under the covers, desolate, dreading the day before me. My head throbbed with dull pain. I slid out of bed and went to the basin to splash my face with cold water. Then I crossed to the window and drew back the curtains.

The sky was cloudless, rain-washed, the delicate pale blue of summer harebells. The grounds of Deer's Leap seemed to shimmer, every blade of grass, every tuft of heather, every feathery spray of the conifer trees reflecting sunlight from the clinging raindrops. I had seen countless such mornings, mornings when I'd felt thrilled to be alive, when I'd been impatient to have breakfast over and get out into the soft, tangy air that blew in over the ridge of downs straight off the sea.

Today, without interest, I pulled on slacks and a sweater and hastily brushed my hair. I put on make-up only because Madeleine might notice if I didn't. On this dreadful day, for her sake, I had to cling to normality in every little way I could.

The house was silent, except for the sounds that came from the kitchen. When I entered, Freda Aiken and Mrs. Cramp at once broke off their conversation and stared at me. I said good morning, and Mrs. Cramp sniffed.

"What's good about it, I'd like to know! It's not very nice for me, all this going on, and everyone knowing that I work here! I've been wondering if I ought to give my notice."

I was in no mood to placate Mrs. Cramp this morning. She was a gossipmonger, and I knew she must be loving every minute, storing up tales to tell when she went back home to the village each afternoon.

I said curtly, "I'm sure Mrs. Karel would be very sorry to lose you. But if you feel you must leave . . ."

She shot me a killing look. "I might at that!" Her eyes swiveled to Freda Aiken, as if sharing a private joke, then she glanced back at me. "You made a proper fool of yourself, didn't you, going chasing around all over the Continent after your uncle? That Belle Forsyth put you in your place by all accounts!"

"What do you mean?" I asked feebly.

"Don't make out as if you didn't know. It's all in the paper this morning for everyone to read."

She pointed to a newspaper that lay open on the kitchen table. I was confronted with a picture of myself, hands coming up to shield my face—one of those snapped in the lobby of the Hôtel des Alpes-Maritimes in Nice. Beside me stood Brett.

Somehow, in all the turmoil of the past twenty-four hours, I'd forgotten about the newspapers. There was a full, maliciously slanted report of my encounter with Belle in Geneva. I felt sickened as I saw they had even included a veiled reference to her spiteful remarks about Madeleine.

I was aware of the two women watching me, getting pleasure out of my distress. But if they knew the real truth, perhaps they wouldn't be so unfeeling.

"It's horrible!" I said faintly. "The papers have no right to print things like that."

"Isn't it true, then?" asked Freda with pretended innocence.

I didn't bother to answer her. I'd come to the kitchen intending to make myself a cup of coffee. But I had lost interest now.

"Is my aunt awake yet?" I asked.

Freda shook her head. "And she won't be for some time. She's got to sleep off that extra pill."

"Yes. I'd forgotten."

I left the kitchen and went in search of Rudi, but he was nowhere around. I guessed that he must have gone through to see the Warrenders. Caterina was certain to have told Sir Ralph what the morning papers were saying, and I shuddered to think how they'd be reacting to the sordid blaze of publicity. No doubt they would blame me for keeping it stirred up.

Would Rudi pass on to them all that I had said? Would he tell them I believed my uncle was dead and that the man I had seen in Geneva was an impostor? But how could he tell them all that without mentioning Brett's part in the plot?

Anyway, Rudi himself thought I was mistaken. He had made that clear.

I lacked the courage to face Sir Ralph, to see the condemnation in his blind eyes. I didn't really feel up to facing Rudi, either. Never in my whole life had I felt more alone than at this moment. I *was* alone.

Paradoxically, the realization brought with it a curious sense of peace, of calm determination. Upon my shoulders, now, rested the sole responsibility for Madeleine—a trust I had inherited from Alexis. It was a sacred trust that I would carry out to the best of my ability. Madeleine would have to be told the truth as I saw it myself, and I must protect her and help her through her grief. I must help her to understand that whatever cruel things might be said and written about

Alexis, she had a right to be proud of him—in death just as she had always been during his lifetime.

And I had another sacred trust: to vindicate the name of Alexis Karel in the eyes of the world, however long it took me. I owed my uncle that.

I went upstairs at once to Madeleine's room, opening the door quietly. She lay in a deep sleep, and I couldn't bring myself to rouse her. A sound behind me on the landing made me turn. Freda Aiken stood there, frowning at me.

"I told you your aunt was asleep, Miss Fleming."

"Yes, but I hoped she might have wakened by now. I want to see her just as soon as she does."

"Very well. I'll let you know."

I wondered whether to go along to my own bedroom and wait there. But somehow the idea was almost claustrophobic. I needed to get out in the fresh air.

"I'll be outside," I told Freda. "Not far away— down by the lake. Would you mind giving me a call?"

"Very well," she said again, stonily.

The grounds at Deer's Leap were as full of poignant memories for me as the house itself. Crossing the terrace, I recalled how Alexis and I used to play energetic games of shuttlecock on the lawn—regrettably it was too uneven to have the makings of a tennis court.

As I went down the flight of stone steps, the winter jasmine flowering against the wall brought back the year my uncle had inveigled me into helping him prune the straggly, overgrown bushes. Afterward, we were afraid that in our novice enthusiasm we'd been too drastic—until February came around and the delicate pale-yellow blossoms appeared in greater profusion than ever.

The jasmine needed pruning again, I thought sadly.

I followed the wide, sloping path that curved down to the lake. Only a yard from my feet, a brilliantly plumaged cock pheasant rose out of the dead bracken in sudden panic flight, startling me, as always, with its wildly flapping wings and raucous shrieks.

The old dinghy was still there, I noticed, drawn up above the waterline on the tiny pebble beach. Probably it had not been used since the last time I had rowed upon the lake, an age ago. Now, the dinghy was awash with last night's rain. I tipped it on its side to drain.

The rustic seat by the willow tree had already steamed dry in the warm sunshine. I sat and gazed into the lake's calm water, seeing the dark mirrored shapes of the conifers that fringed the farther bank. Suddenly, I saw a movement among the still reflections. A fallow doe! I looked up quickly. It was a long time since I had seen one at Deer's Leap, a long time since I had sat quietly enough. Even from across the water she seemed to sense the lifting of my head and vanished among the trees, swiftly, with hardly a sound.

Timid creature!

But wasn't I just as timid? Dawdling here on the pretext of waiting for Madeleine to waken. In truth, I was thankful for the delay which postponed the moment I dreaded.

With sudden decision I rose to my feet and started walking up the path, back toward the house. I didn't hurry, but I made myself walk on steadily without pause.

I raised my eyes to look up at the rear facade of Deer's Leap, so belovedly familiar. In the clear, bright sunlight the old house took on many hues. The gray stone walls were tawny yellow in places where lichen grew, and the dark-green clinging ivy made a striking contrast. Sparrows flitted in and out, already busy with their nest building. Above the parapet, dotted among the jumbled peaks and valleys of the roof, soared tall chimneys built of terracotta bricks.

The long casement windows of Madeleine's room were open to the soft morning air, and through them I saw a flash of white. A quick, darting movement. Madeleine came flying to the window, standing framed there with her arms outstretched, calling. But it was not my name she called.

"Alexis! Alexis!"

She appeared to be clambering up onto the low sill. Behind her, I saw Freda Aiken, trying to hold on to her, trying to drag her back to safety.

With a horrified gasp, I started to run.

I could see Madeleine struggling with Freda, fighting with a desperate strength to shake off her restraining arms. Then suddenly she gave a violent jerk, diving forward, plunging into space. I heard a long piercing scream as she fell.

Frantic with terror, I raced across the lawn and up the terrace steps.

Madeleine lay quite still, her poor crumpled body like a broken bird. I knew without a doubt that she was dead. I knelt beside her and lifted her head, cradling it in my arms.

Chapter Sixteen

The hours that followed were a confused blur of time.

Dimly, I remember Freda Aiken reaching Madeleine only a second after I did. And the others came quickly —Rudi first, then Sir Ralph and Caterina, gathering around us. We were all in a shocked daze, numb with disbelief. Such a dreadful thing could not have happened! And then came the anguished questioning. What had made Madeleine do it—why, why, why?

Freda Aiken, when she'd checked in vain for Madeleine's pulse and knew beyond all hope that she was dead, had broken down completely. She seemed to blame herself.

"I heard her scream," she sobbed, "and I ran to her room. She was already out of bed, going to the window, distraught. For some reason she was crying her husband's name. I tried to stop her, tried to hold her back, but she was so strong! She tore herself out of my arms, and suddenly she was gone. Oh, dear God!"

Later, in Madeleine's room, we found the answer. A tabloid newspaper, open at a center page, was lying on the bed. The picture of me, shielding my face. The story of my encounter with Belle, the cruel innuendo that Madeleine was out of her mind and would be better off in a mental home.

Mrs. Cramp's paper! But how had it reached Madeleine's room?

Could it have been put there by Freda Aiken, out of malice, as a sick joke? It would explain Freda's present desperation. Or had Mrs. Cramp, going up to vacuum the room and finding Madeleine still asleep, somehow left the newspaper there? Accidentally or vindictively?

Mrs. Cramp fiercely denied that she had been to my aunt's room at all that morning. "*I* don't know how the paper got there," she said doggedly. "I brought it from home. I never even took it out of the kitchen."

But now that Madeleine was dead, neither of them would dare to confess. It was a dark enigma, and in all probability it would remain so.

The doctor came quickly in response to Rudi's urgent phone call. And then the police. We were told that of course there would have to be an inquest. Wearily, I answered the questions, dozens of questions. Yes, I had actually seen it happen. I had watched my aunt fall to her death. I was in the garden, coming back to see her, to talk to her, to tell her . . .

"To tell her what, Miss Fleming?"

I hesitated. "I was going to tell her that she would never see my uncle again. I had come to the decision that I couldn't put it off any longer."

The police inspector was a thickset, quiet-speaking man. He raised his shaggy eyebrows.

"Why hadn't you told her long ago, Miss Fleming? Instead, your aunt learned about her husband in a crueler way. How do you think that copy of the newspaper might have got into her room? Could Mrs. Karel have fetched it from the kitchen herself?"

I didn't know! I didn't know! I only knew that Madeleine was dead. Somehow, I controlled myself.

"Normally," I said huskily, "my aunt never looked at a newspaper or listened to the radio. She was always rather timid. You see, she had been through a great deal when she lived in Czechoslovakia. News of any

kind of violence upset her, frightened her." Finally
they left me alone.

The morning passed with agonizing slowness. Caterina was wonderfully kind, comforting me, trying to
coax me to eat something. But I couldn't eat. I seem to
remember swallowing some hot tea.

Reporters kept arriving at the house. Sir Ralph dealt
with them, keeping them away from me. I was grateful to him.

In the afternoon I went upstairs to be alone with
Madeleine. Her body had been laid upon the bed, and
in death her face looked strangely calm and serene,
the lids closed upon her lovely golden eyes. I felt I
needed these last quiet moments of contact with my
aunt. And through her, with the uncle I had loved so
dearly.

I moved about the room, imprinting every detail
upon my memory. Propped on the easel beside the
window, I saw her latest painting, almost finished. A
work in oils.

Unlike her delicate watercolors, it made a violent
impression, the paint laid on the canvas in thick bold
strokes, crude in their intensity. But even so it held a
kind of tenderness. A baby, lying asleep in its cradle.
Until, looking closer, I understood its true meaning. A
baby laid out in its tiny coffin! The baby she had never
had. The baby that was born dead.

I lingered in the room as daylight faded, unwilling to
leave. It would seem like desertion. There was nothing
I could do for Madeleine now except to stay with her,
filling my thoughts with memories of her.

After the clear fine winter day, an afternoon mist
was closing down. As I stood by the window, gazing
out, the shapes gradually softened, growing indistinct.
The lawn, the lake, the trees merged slowly into an
overall grayness.

It was then that Brett found me.

I heard his voice from the doorway and swung
around, startled, suddenly pierced through with fear.

"Gail! I came the moment I heard about Madeleine."

I stared at him, not speaking, not moving.

He came into the room and stopped at the foot of the bed, looking down at Madeleine, silently shaking his head. Then he turned to me and held out his hand.

"Come downstairs now, Gail. I want to talk to you."

Still I didn't move. Brett's hand dropped to his side.

"Do you think I'm some sort of monster?" he said bitterly. "Do you imagine that I'm going to try and strangle you?"

My throat felt dry, and I couldn't speak.

His voice gentled. "We can't talk here, Gail, and there's a lot to be said. Come downstairs."

I hesitated a few moments longer. Then, moving stiffly, I walked past him and went out of the room. He followed me, closing the door with quiet care.

We went down to the Winter Parlor. Rudi was there. He looked at me anxiously.

"Would you mind leaving us for a while, Rudi," said Brett. "I know you understand."

Rudi glanced at me swiftly, his dark eyes troubled, questioning. I gave him a tiny nod. Brett could not harm me here, in his father's house. Anyway, would he want to harm me now? As far as he was concerned, it was all over. I had abandoned my search for Alexis. He could not know of my determination to go on until I had exposed the truth.

Rudi was looking at Brett as he spoke, but I knew his words were really meant for me. "If you want me, I'll be just outside."

After he had left us, we both remained standing, I beside the sofa, Brett by the fireplace. Ten feet apart.

He said, "I heard the news just before noon. I couldn't believe it at first—and then I knew I had to come home and be with you. I was in Geneva."

"In Geneva?"

He nodded, his eyes fixed upon me steadily.

"I was snowed in at the *mas* and had a terrible job getting away. I was mad as hell with you. I thought you'd done a skip the same as you did in Palma. After you drove off, I got straight through on the phone to Dougal's hotel in Cannes. He'd already left, but I learned that just a few minutes before he'd put a call through to the Shackleton number, so I knew he must have spoken to you. They were able to tell me that he was flying to Geneva, and as soon as I could get myself back to civilization, I headed straight there. But it took me the devil of a time."

"You . . . you saw Dougal?" I asked faintly.

"Oh yes, I saw Dougal. And he told me." Brett's face creased into an expression of pain. "Gail, how could you possibly imagine I'd want to harm you? Let alone—"

"You wanted to stop me reaching Alexis," I said chokily. "I mean, that man who was *pretending* to be Alexis."

Brett took a pace toward me, and instinctively I moved back.

"When Dougal first told me the fantastic things you'd been saying, Gail—about your uncle being murdered and the whole thing being an elaborate Communist plot to bring discredit on the name Alexis Karel —I thought the same as him. I thought you'd gone out of your mind from the strain of it all, clutching at any wild theory that would let you keep your faith in Alexis. But then I got to thinking."

Suddenly breathless, I waited for him to go on. The room was silent, the whole house very still. Brett glanced away fleetingly, then his eyes returned to me.

"Gail, I'm beginning more and more to think you must be right. So many details seem to fit. You insisted all along that the way this man's been acting is completely out of character for Alexis—running off with Belle Forsyth, staying at those luxury hotels, going out of his way to attract publicity. And there's not a shadow of doubt that the Communists would dearly like to discredit Alexis Karel, if they could."

A pulse was beating in my throat. The room, everything around me, was slowly dissolving into a haze. Only Brett's face stood out sharp and clear. If Brett believed in me, it meant . . .

He went on, "I decided my best plan was to hang on in Geneva for a bit. Then, wherever that pair turned up next, I could rush straight off and confront them. I'd be able to tell whether it was Alexis or not, and that would sort it out one way or the other. But I've got a hunch that if you're right, Gail, and he *is* a phony, then we've seen the last of them."

"We have!" I burst out. "I'm positive they won't make another appearance. The Communists have achieved what they set out to achieve."

Brett said grimly, "If those bastards have murdered Alexis, then I swear to God I won't let them get away with it!"

"They did kill him, Brett. I know they did!"

He came to me, taking hold of my hands, and I didn't flinch away. Brett looked into my eyes, sadly, searchingly.

"Gail, I was shattered when Dougal told me the rest of it—that you believed I was one of *them* and had been trying to kill you. I thought it was some sort of stupid joke. And then I thought again about the strange way you'd acted after your fall—the way you'd *looked* at me, as if I scared you to death—and then driving off in the car like someone crazy. But *why,* darling? It hurts like hell. Whatever put such a monstrous idea into your head?"

I was wondering the very same thing myself. As I looked into Brett's eyes, seeing his pain and bewilderment, it seemed inconceivable now that I could ever have suspected him. And yet . . . there were so many things still unexplained.

"Brett, there *was* a man up on that crag! He called out for help, in *English*. It was just when I was turning back because I realized the path was dangerously icy. I heard him shouting, and that made me press on. I was hurrying to him and suddenly I slipped and fell over the edge. By some miracle I was saved by a bush only a few feet down, and I was able to scramble up to the path again. Otherwise, I'd have been killed!"

Brett's fingers tightened on mine. "I had no idea! You didn't tell me it was so bad." He shook his head slowly, thoughtfully. "All the same, Gail, I still think it

was just the wind you heard. But even if you did believe it was a man, why *me?*"

"I didn't see who else it could have been. Besides,
there was the footprint."

"Footprint?" he asked, mystified.

"In a patch of snow, up above the path—the imprint
of *your* shoe! I recognized the pattern of the tread."

"Well, that's easily explained. I'd climbed up to the
top of the crag the afternoon before, while you were
having a sleep."

"Oh, Brett! I didn't think of that." Suddenly I felt
the need to justify myself, to show him I'd had some
rational foundation for my fantastic ideas. "You see,
coming after the other things it all seemed to add up
and click into place. *You* could have been responsible
for every one of them."

"What other things?" asked Brett sharply.

"Well, the car that nearly ran me down in Palma.
I'm convinced it wasn't a drunk or anything like that.
It was *deliberate*—and I remembered how you talked
me out of going to the police. And smaller things, too.
Like in Nice, when there was that car blocking our
Renault in the hotel garage, delaying us so that we just
missed seeing Alexis before he checked out. I wanted
to take a taxi, but you said no. And that stupid night
porter took ages sorting out the right key, so I argued
you must have bribed him to be so slow. And at London Airport, just when I was starting out, someone
snatched my handbag. Without my passport, I couldn't
have left the country. Luckily, there was this American. He was marvelous. He saw it happen and managed to grab the thief and make him drop my bag."

As he listened to me, Brett's expression had slowly
changed, and now his brow was creased in a heavy
frown.

"It does seem to add up, Gail. Someone—or some
organization—was pretty desperate to prevent you
from catching up with Belle and the man she's with.
It looks as if they must have had people tailing you
from the moment you first set out after Alexis, and
they took every opportunity they could find to stop

you. But it had to appear accidental." He took a quick, angry breath. "And to think I was with you the whole time and allowed it to happen! A lot of use I was when you needed me."

"Brett, I still don't really understand. *Why* did you insist on coming with me to Majorca? And then sticking with me? I kept wondering."

"Don't you really know, Gail? Can't you guess? You see, I reckoned you were in for disillusionment when you saw Alexis. I was sure you'd be badly hurt, and I wanted to be there to pick up the pieces. God forgive me, though, I never realized . . . I never dreamed for a second that your life was in danger."

Suddenly, as if without conscious thought from either of us, I was in his arms. Brett held me close and I buried my face in his shoulder. Tenderly, he stroked my hair.

"We're going to get to the bottom of this, Gail," he whispered. "It's got to be brought out into the open, and I won't let up until it is!"

Beneath his gentleness with me I was aware of the anger in him, matching my own anger. But I felt an overwhelming sense of relief, too, a surging joy at knowing that I was no longer alone. I had Brett again.

Chapter Seventeen

Everything seemed to lead back to Belle Forsyth. She was the key figure—a figure shrouded in mystery.

Brett said, "I've got a feeling that if we could once get a lead on Belle, we might begin to find some answers. How did she ever come to get a job here, Gail?"

I shook my head, feeling a flush of guilt. It had been just at the time of my break-up with Brett, and I had been too absorbed in my misery to question the circumstances of Belle Forsyth's coming. When I next went home for the weekend, Belle was already an accepted member of the household. Like everyone else, I had thought her eminently suitable as a companion for my aunt.

"I suppose I just assumed Alexis had arranged it through an agency or something," I said. "But we could ask Rudi. He would know."

It was late in the evening, but I don't believe that anybody at Deer's Leap was considering going to bed. We were all of us still in a state of shock, grieving for Madeleine.

I guessed that Sir Ralph and Caterina were inwardly raging against the man they believed had driven Madeleine to take her own life. Brett and I hadn't attempted to undeceive them. What was the use of removing one horror only to substitute a more sinister one in their minds? Time enough, when Brett and I could find some positive proof to vindicate Alexis.

With a sense of dread, I knew what this would entail. We would have to find some clear evidence that my uncle was dead. Murdered! I was certain of it myself. And I thought that by now Brett believed it as surely as I did.

And Rudi—what did *he* believe?

I hated having to admit to Brett what Rudi had told me earlier, but there must be no concealment between us now.

"Rudi thinks—he says he's *sure* that Alexis and Belle were having an affair here at Deer's Leap long before they went away together."

Brett turned his head, staring at me. "When did he tell you this?"

"When I got back during the night. He said that he'd known for some time, but there was nothing he could do about it."

Frowning deeply to himself, Brett said, "If it's true, Gail, it puts a very different complexion on the whole thing. We'll have to start wondering if we aren't on the wrong tack after all."

"No!" The word jerked out of me, almost in panic. I couldn't bear to lose Brett's support now. "The man with Belle in Geneva—I *know* it wasn't Alexis. I actually saw him! And . . . and remember all those other things—all the attempts to stop me reaching him."

I was filled with fear because of my own inner uncertainty. Ever since Rudi had told me about Alexis and Belle, I'd felt this tiny rift of doubt. In that penthouse suite in Geneva, I'd been certain the man was not Alexis. But now, with only my memory to guide me, only my instincts, could I really be so positive? The question tormented me.

Brett said, "We'd better have a talk with Rudi and see if he can shed any further light."

Rudi was in the Oak Room. We found him sitting behind the typewriter staring blankly into space. Brett came straight to the point.

"Gail has just this minute told me what you were saying about Alexis and Belle having some sort of affair. What makes you think so?"

Rudi rose slowly to his feet. The light from the desk lamp, striking up through the parchment shade, caught his face from underneath so that his eyes were lost in shadow.

"It's quite true," he said defensively. "They were. I told Gail because I thought she ought to know. She'd got a wild idea in her head that the man she saw in Geneva wasn't Alexis."

Brett reached out his arm and drew me against him. "Gail had several wild ideas in her head. But this about it not being Alexis—I think she may well be right there."

I heard Rudi's sharp intake of breath. He sat down again, heavily, and put his hands to his face. After a long pause, he spoke in a low, unhappy voice.

"Gail thinks that if she is right . . . if it *wasn't* Alexis, then we must assume that Alexis is dead." Rudi lifted his head and looked at Brett. "Would you rather believe that Alexis is dead?"

"It's not a question of what we *want* to believe," said Brett roughly. "We're trying to get at the truth."

"I've told you the truth. Alexis and Belle were having an affair. They were lovers!"

"But what evidence have you for saying that?" insisted Brett.

"The evidence of my own eyes. She was often in his bedroom at night."

"How do you know that?"

"Because several times in the early hours I happened to see her, just after she'd come out of his room. She looked terribly embarrassed and tried to cover up. And once, I remember, her own bedroom door was left wide open and no light on. I searched for her, but she was nowhere to be seen. She must have been in Alexis's room then."

"What were *you* doing up and about in the early hours of the morning?" demanded Brett.

Rudi was frowning. "Usually I sleep soundly. But sometimes, when I get to remembering the past, I find I cannot sleep."

"Alexis was the same," I put in swiftly. "He would often be up half the night, reading."

Brett's eyes turned again to Rudi. "Did you see any other signs that there was something going on between them?"

"There were a hundred things. I noticed the way Belle used to look at him, a sort of secret excitement in her eyes. It was unmistakable. I suppose a woman can never conceal her emotions when she looks at the man who is her lover."

Brett asked sharply, "And what about the way Alexis looked at Belle?"

Rudi lifted his shoulders. "I suppose deceit comes more easily to a man."

"That's a matter of opinion!" said Brett. "Anything else?"

"Isn't that enough? If you had seen the two of them together day after day these past months, you'd be as convinced as I am." Rudi hesitated, then added quickly, "There *was* something. I remember one morning . . . Alexis had gone to London soon after breakfast. I went up to his room for some papers he'd left there, and I saw Belle's silver locket—you know the one I mean, Gail. She always wore it around her neck. It was on the bedside table in Alexis's bedroom. Of course, I didn't touch it, and later, at lunchtime, Belle's hand went to her throat as she suddenly realized it was missing. She made some excuse to leave the table, and when she returned she was wearing it again."

"That's all, is it?" said Brett. "That's what you based your supposition on?"

"Well, yes."

There was a moment's pause, then Brett said, "You realize there are two possible explanations for all this. The first that Alexis and Belle were lovers, the second that they weren't but that Belle wanted you to *think* they were. Every single thing you've mentioned could have been just an act put on by Belle for your special benefit, Rudi."

My pulse rate quickened. I dared not snatch too quickly at an explanation I longed to believe.

"According to what you've told us," Brett went on, "there's nothing to suggest that Alexis was the least bit interested in Belle in that sense. It was the way *she* used to look at *him*. *She* who'd apparently just come out of *his* bedroom. I noticed that you didn't say you actually saw her *coming* out—you just assumed she had, because she looked so embarrassed. And she seems to have chosen just the moments when she knew you were around to see. *Several* times, you said. Doesn't that strike you as a remarkable coincidence? And that locket incident—mark that it was on a day when Alexis had gone to London, so Belle could easily have planted the locket after he'd left. And possibly taken up some papers she knew you'd be needing, to make sure you went up there and saw it."

I couldn't contain my excitement. "Oh yes, Brett, I'm sure that's it. Everything fits."

Rudi sat with his face in his hands, and we stood watching him. At length he lifted his head. "You're quite right! There wasn't a single occasion when Alexis showed any sign. It was always Belle. Oh God," he groaned, his eyes suddenly sharpened with tragedy. "I should have realized . . . You understand what this means? They really have murdered him!"

Brett said slowly, quietly, "It's terrible, but I know which way the Alexis I remember would have wished it himself. He'd rather have lost his life any day than be dishonored, than have all that he's worked for over the years discredited. No, Gail is right, I'm convinced of it."

I squeezed his arm in gratitude, and Brett glanced down at me with a sad little smile.

"I can't take any of the credit, Gail. It was you, and it puts the rest of us to shame. You were the only one who had faith in Alexis. You never doubted him, however black things looked."

This wasn't quite as true as Brett believed. There had come a point—after that humiliating scene with Belle, in those frantic minutes before I discovered that the man with her was not Alexis at all—when I faced complete disillusionment. But perhaps, in the circumstances, I could not really be blamed.

"Alexis and I had always been so close," I whispered. "He was more like a father to me than an uncle."

Rudi sat with his head drooped. "I looked upon Alexis almost as a father, too, yet I was ready to think the worst of him. I shall never forgive myself, Gail. *Never!*" He jumped to his feet and began striding about the room, a man in torment.

My heart was wrenched in pity for him. I knew how much he had loved my uncle. Forced to flee his native land, separated forever from his only living relatives—his sister and her family in Karlovy Vary—Rudi had, through Alexis, found a whole new meaning for his life. It was terrible for him to go on believing that some negligence on his part had allowed Alexis to be seized and killed.

"Rudi, you don't need to blame yourself. What could *you* have done to stop this from happening?"

Leaving Brett's side, I went to Rudi, touching his arm in compassion. To my surprise, he jerked himself away.

"I don't deserve your pity, Gail!" he said in a bitter voice.

Brett cut in, "Let's not talk about blame. It doesn't get us anywhere. Our job now is to discover the truth. It's one thing for us three to feel certain we know what happened, but it will be quite a different matter to convince other people. What we've got to do is find some real, solid evidence that Alexis was murdered. So far it's just guesswork. Let's start at the beginning. Exactly how did Belle Forsyth work herself into a job here? Did she come from an employment agency?"

We both looked at Rudi. He made an effort to pull himself together. "Yes, we've got to try and be practical. But I'm afraid I can't help about Belle. I've no idea where she came from. Alexis merely told me one day that he'd found the perfect nurse-companion for Madeleine, and I was delighted." He gave me an apologetic shrug. "I know it sounds odd not to have asked Alexis for any details. But I was up to my eyes at the time—working on the indexing of the book. As you can imagine, with so many cross-references it was a complicated job."

"When was it Alexis told you about Belle?" asked Brett. "What were the circumstances? For example, had he been up to London that day? Could he somehow have met her there?"

Rudi hesitated, but in the end he made a helpless gesture with his hands.

"I can't remember clearly. I think we were here in the study, and I think . . . yes, I'm pretty sure that Alexis had just read a letter. Perhaps it was from Belle."

"If so, presumably you had to answer it, make an appointment for her to come for an interview or something?"

Rudi looked from Brett to me. I could sense his desperate anxiety to be of some help. But in the end he could only shake his head.

"Alexis fixed it up entirely by himself. He just told me she was coming the following week. And of course, when she did come, she really seemed ideal. Madeleine was immensely taken with her."

I closed my eyes, remembering bitterly how my poor

aunt had been deceived by Belle Forsyth's treacherous charm. Even a few hours before Madeleine's death, when I'd talked to her in the middle of the night, she had been wondering when her dear Belle would be coming back.

"Did Belle have any friends?" Brett continued. "Any contacts at all?"

Again Rudi shook his head. "The Communists will have covered their tracks well. Any line you try to follow about Belle Forsyth will only end in a blank wall." His voice cracked. "I know them! They will go to endless trouble to achieve their aims."

Brett said crisply, "I can understand how you feel, Rudi, but a defeatist attitude won't get us anywhere. The only way I know of winning is to keep pressing on even when things look utterly hopeless. As Gail did from the very beginning. As I'm going to do from now on."

It was very late when at last Brett persuaded me to go up to bed. The doctor had given me a pill to take, so at least I knew I would be able to sleep.

We parted at the foot of the staircase before Brett went through to the other wing of the house. He held me to him briefly, kissing my forehead. Then he let me go.

"Gail, I've come to a decision. I'm going to go ahead with the film about Alexis. I'm going to finish it. Some day—very soon, I hope—it will be needed. I want it to make a fitting memorial to Alexis Karel."

Chapter Eighteen

I heard the cheerful whistle of the newspaper boy as I came downstairs the next morning. His bicycle slithered to a racing stop on the gravel. The folded copy of the *Times* appeared through the letterbox and fell to the floor with a thud.

For a few moments I stood staring at it, as if it was something contaminated. Then I bent and picked it up, scanning through it quickly.

Madeleine's death was reported with brief details. The paragraph went on to say that Dr. Alexis Karel had not been seen or heard of since having a short interview with his niece, Miss Gail Fleming, at a hotel in Geneva a few days before. That was all.

I left the paper on the console table in the hall and went to the kitchen to get myself some coffee. A big cupful, hot and milky, slowly brought me back to life. I even found the appetite to eat a buttered crispbread. To my relief, Mrs. Cramp hadn't turned up yet.

I heard Brett calling my name and went out to the hall to meet him. He smiled at me, his eyes searching my face.

"You look tired, darling. Did you sleep?"

"A bit too heavily. I'm not used to taking pills."

"Let's hope you never will be. Have you seen the *Times* yet?"

"Yes, just now. It doesn't say much."

"I know, but some of the popular papers have really gone to town—as you'd expect. Look, Gail, I can't stop. I just came through to tell you that I'm off to London."

"To London?"

"Yes, I must go today. You see, things have rather piled up while we were away."

I felt a sudden chill. I'd completely overlooked the fact that Brett had a job to do. Foolishly, I had pictured him being here with me at Deer's Leap, working together to find the answer to Alexis's disappearance.

I said dispiritedly, "When will I see you again?"

"Oh, sometime later today. I want to restart work on the film right away."

I felt better at once. Brett wasn't forsaking me.

"Caterina asked me to say she hopes you'll join them for lunch, Gail. You will, won't you?"

"Yes, of course. It's kind of her to ask me . . . in the circumstances."

"Gail, you mustn't think that! My father is very upset—naturally. But not with *you!*"

"All the same, I'm part of it all. A continual reminder."

Brett stood hesitating for a moment, as if he felt torn. Then he said quickly, "I really must get going. There's a planning meeting at ten-thirty, and I've barely time to make it." He bent and kissed me swiftly on my cheek. "I won't be gone all that long. I reckon that Elspeth and I should arrive about teatime."

Elspeth! I had completely overlooked her, too.

Since Brett's return last night when we had talked, I had believed that he and I were together once more after these long months of separation. In my newfound feeling of warm security I had shut my eyes to the part Elspeth Vane played in his life. Elspeth directed nearly every one of the films Brett made, and often they traveled together, both in England and abroad. When they were actually filming, Brett saw Elspeth every day. And at night, too? Was the former relationship between them still continuing?

After Brett had gone, I went in search of Rudi and found him in the Oak Room. He was sorting through some papers in a halfhearted fashion.

"Hello, Gail. There isn't really anything for me to do, but somehow I can't just do nothing. So I'm collating Alexis's notes. One day, perhaps, someone will be interested in them."

It was the same as Brett had said about the film.

I thought how ill Rudi looked. I wished I could say or do something that would ease his feelings of guilt.

I walked over to the window and stood staring out through the leaded panes. This morning the sun was shining again, mocking us with its cheerful golden brilliance. Against the pale-blue sky, the tips of the conifer trees stood up like an edging of black lace. I was thankful that the Oak Room looked out to the rock gardens and not to the terrace where Madeleine had fallen.

"Rudi, I've been thinking—there's no reason for Freda Aiken to stay any longer. We could pay her off and suggest she leave right away."

Rudi said heavily, "Is that a hint, Gail? Do you mean that you'd like *me* to leave Deer's Leap, too?"

I spun around to face him. "No, of course I didn't mean anything of the kind! Later . . . well, I don't know what will happen. Obviously I shan't be staying on here myself indefinitely. But please don't think of leaving, not for the time being. I need you here. With Freda Aiken, though, it's altogether different. There's really nothing more for her to do. Perhaps I'm being unjust to her, but every time I see the woman I can't help wondering . . ."

"Wondering what?"

"Well, it could so easily have been Freda who left the newspaper for Madeleine to see. I wouldn't put a thing like that past her—there's a sort of spiteful streak in her that would think it amusing. Obviously though, she'd never have expected such a terrible consequence. If it *was* Freda, then that would explain why she's so dreadfully upset."

Rudi was staring down at his hands, gripped tightly together on the desk. "If you feel like that, Gail, I suppose it's best to get rid of her at once. I don't much care for Freda myself, I admit, and I wouldn't be sorry to see the back of her." He hesitated, looking uneasy. "All the same, I'd hate having to tell her to her face that she's got to get out."

"I wasn't expecting you to, Rudi," I said quickly. "That's *my* job. I'll go and tell her right away."

Freda Aiken was in her bedroom and opened the door to my knock.

"Oh . . . it's you, Miss Fleming. I was just . . ."

Though it was nearly ten o'clock, she was still in her dressing gown. She looked so dejected that I couldn't help feeling sorry for her. But believing what I did, remembering that she'd shown no human kindness toward Madeleine in the short time she'd been my aunt's nurse, I hardened my heart.

"I just wanted a word with you, Miss Aiken. You'll understand that there's really no point in you staying on at Deer's Leap any longer, so I thought . . ." I saw her eyes widen in alarm. She started to make some protest, and I added hastily, "Naturally your salary will be honored—whatever the arrangement was. But there's nothing for you to do here now, and you could be working somewhere else, or having a holiday."

Her face seemed to crumble up, and she looked as if she was going to burst into tears.

"Oh, Miss Fleming, please don't send me away. I . . . I've got to stay nearby, to give evidence at the inquest, and I . . . well, I'd hate to have to lodge with *strangers*."

It seemed extraordinary to hear Freda Aiken speaking as if we at Deer's Leap were her friends. But it was true that I had forgotten about her being needed for the inquest.

"Oh well," I said awkwardly, "in that case I suppose—"

"Then I can stay?" Her face brightened at once. "Oh, you are kind! I'm so grateful. I've had a dreadful night, Miss Fleming. I couldn't sleep at all for thinking. I mean, your poor aunt was supposed to be my responsibility. She was put in my charge."

Amazingly, I found myself defending her, trying to bring reassurance to this woman I disliked so much.

"You mustn't torture yourself, Miss Aiken. You couldn't be expected to spend every single moment with her."

After I had left Freda, I decided on an impulse to have a look in the bedroom Belle Forsyth had used. Just possibly I might find some clue there.

It was, as always, immaculately tidy. I stood in the middle of the blue carpet, staring about me, reluctant to touch anything that Belle had handled. But I forced the feeling down.

I was opening the top drawer of the tallboy when it struck me that I must be careful not to disturb anything. One day there might be a full-scale criminal investigation.

The contents of the drawer were entirely impersonal. They might have belonged to anyone. Odds and ends of lipstick, face cream, and powder, a bottle of skin lotion, some French Fern bath cubes—all well-known makes that could be bought at any pharmacy.

The unexotic, everyday beauty items that fitted the image of Belle Forsyth—nurse and companion. And a small pile of handkerchiefs, all plain white hemstitched, unmarked in any way.

I closed the drawer and passed to the next one down. It contained chain-store underwear, neatly folded. Several pairs of tights. In the bottom drawer there were blouses and sweaters, all like a million other women possessed.

What exactly was I looking for? I didn't know. Just something, *anything,* that would point to Belle's true character—give a lead, perhaps, about where she had come from. Just a tiny shred of solid evidence.

On the bedside table was a paperback, a collection of modern verse. I flicked through the pages, expecting nothing, finding nothing. I went across and opened the heavy oak wardrobe. There were a couple of wool dresses on hangers, a red jersey suit, a gaberdine raincoat, two or three skirts. A black umbrella, neatly rolled, was looped over a hook. I examined every item without hope. Manufacturers' labels told me nothing. The pockets of the suit and raincoat were empty.

Clean white paper lined the bottom of the wardrobe. But in one corner, at the back, it wasn't lying quite flat. As I automatically bent and smoothed it down with my hand, I felt a ridge of something like a piece of thick cardboard.

Suddenly excited, I drew the lining paper back. I saw a large buff envelope, torn open along one edge. The name and address were typewritten—*Miss Belle Forsyth, Deer's Leap* . . . It contained photographs. I shook them out, spreading them on the carpet.

There were five altogether, postcard size, all of them similar—but none exactly the same—as the picture of Belle I'd seen in the newspaper. The changed Belle, with her hair cascading down. In one photograph the tip of her tongue showed teasingly between her lips. In another her shoulders were drawn back to reveal the outline of her breasts through the thin silk of her dress.

A series of six, obviously, and one photograph had

been carefully chosen and passed into the hands of a newspaper. The photograph that best portrayed Belle Forsyth in the way it was wanted to portray her—as a cheaply provocative woman for whom the distinguished Alexis Karel had abandoned his invalid wife.

I picked up the pictures, one by one, examined them, and turned them over. There was no identification, nothing to show where they had come from. I looked again at the envelope, but it was empty.

The postmark was my only clue. It was smudgy, and at first glance I couldn't make it out. I went over to the window, tilting the envelope to catch the sunlight. Against the blue postage stamp I could hardly decipher anything, except, at the bottom, the word *Sussex*. So it had been mailed locally!

The date was completely unreadable, but concentrating on one letter at a time, I decided that the name of the town began with *S* and ended . . . *ven*. I felt triumphant! There was only one place in Sussex that could possibly fit. Seahaven! Someone in Seahaven—the photographer presumably—had sent Belle these prints.

With a sudden rush of excitement I slipped the photos back in the envelope and ran along the corridor to my bedroom. I didn't want to waste time changing. I pulled on a belted raincoat over my slacks and hastily checked my face in the mirror.

Downstairs there was no one around. I collected the spare car keys from the hook by the door and went straight through to the Warrenders' side of the house. Since I didn't know what I hoped to discover in Seahaven, I was glad not to have to explain things to Rudi for the moment.

Caterina happened to be in the staircase hall, arranging early daffodils in a bowl that stood upon the antique marble table.

"Gail, my dear, how are you this morning? You managed to get some rest, I hope?"

"Yes, thank you, Caterina. I—"

"Good morning, Gail!"

Sir Ralph's voice came from behind me. Turning, I saw him standing in the open doorway of the library.

"I gather from my son that he's planning to finish that film of his about Alexis. The Lord knows why. It seems to me the quicker it's all forgotten, the better for everyone. Do *you* understand what's in Brett's mind, Gail?"

He spoke with a kind of suppressed anger, and I guessed there had been sharp disagreement between Brett and his father. I determined to ask Brett, the first moment I could, whether it wasn't time for Sir Ralph and Caterina to be told the truth as we believed it. With the evidence I'd just found of the photographs, and what I hoped to get from the man who had taken them, there was surely enough to convince them we were right.

Perhaps, I thought with wildly flaring hope, it was already enough to convince other people, too!

I restrained my mood of optimism and said quietly, "We don't know the whole story about Alexis yet, Sir Ralph. Brett wants to be ready when the time comes."

"Ready for what?" he asked brusquely. "I'm sorry, my dear—the last thing I want is to upset you, but when I think of Alexis driving your poor aunt to such desperation that she took her own life!"

"The person who left the newspaper in her room is responsible for that," I said.

"Madeleine would have found out sooner or later. It was only a question of time. And it goes to prove what I've maintained all along—that she ought to have been told the truth at the start."

Caterina put out her hand and touched my arm. It was an eloquent gesture, begging me to forbear with her husband.

I bit my lip, swallowing back my anger. "I came to ask you to excuse me from joining you for lunch. It was kind of you to suggest it, but something has cropped up."

Sir Ralph moved forward quickly, his hand groping for me. He found my shoulder and gripped it hard.

"Gail, my dear girl, you must forgive me. I speak my mind too plainly. Please don't take offense. Caterina and I will be delighted to have you lunch with us."

"But it's not that, Sir Ralph. I have to go out—really! I have to go to Seahaven."

Caterina, serving as his eyes, said, "Yes, it is true, Ralph. She's dressed ready to go out. Gail, may I drive you? You shouldn't be on your own today."

I shook my head. "Thanks, Caterina, but I'll be okay. Honestly."

I was actually halfway to Seahaven when the realization struck home with a sickening jolt that the car I was driving, Alexis's ten-year-old Rover, was the one used by Belle and my uncle's double to take them to the airport. And in the car had they also taken Alexis —his body—to wherever it was they had disposed of it?

My heart thudding, I pulled to the side of the road and stopped. For a moment I just sat there, breathing quickly. Perhaps by using the car today I might be destroying vital evidence—if not something obvious, then traces that forensic experts could detect. But I was not the first person to have driven the car since that night. A garageman had brought it back to Deer's Leap from London Airport.

Careful to touch nothing I didn't need to touch, I started to examine the interior—the floor, under the seats, the glove compartment. I found only the untidy paraphernalia Alexis kept—dog-eared maps, a tire pressure gauge, an odd leather glove—nothing with any special significance. I had to force myself to get out and look in the trunk, but it was empty. There were no suspicious looking marks.

Fingerprints? Belle's, of course, would be on the car anyway, because she had been allowed to use it when she wanted to. But her accomplice's prints would be a clue. To preserve any that might still be left, I handled the controls gingerly for the rest of the journey.

The familiar road, almost empty of other traffic, twisted its way to the crest of the downs, then dipped again on the gentler southern slope toward the coast.

Chapter Nineteen

I turned left by the pierhead and parked the car outside a boarded-up ice-cream parlor. Seahaven was battened down for the winter, its forlorn air of neglect emphasized by the bright sunshine.

I knew the post office was in a road at right angles to the seafront, and I went there to check through the classified directory. There were three photographers in the town, I found. I scribbled down their addresses on the back of a telegram form. The first was only two blocks away, in an arcade off the main shopping street. *Arun Studio—Portraits. Weddings. Children a Speciality.* I went in, a buzzer sounding as I trod on the doormat.

"I won't keep you a moment," a man's voice called from the back.

There were specimen prints in several showcases, and I ran my eye over them hoping I might find Belle's face among the dozens on display. But no luck.

The man appeared through a pair of green chenille curtains, slipping on his jacket as he came. He was about fifty, short and fussy, with heavy-framed spectacles.

"I've got some photographs here," I began, "and I wondered if by chance you had taken them. I'm pretty sure it was someone in Seahaven." I slipped the prints from the envelope and held one out to him.

Looking faintly surprised, he gave Belle's picture one glance, then wrinkled his nose in distaste.

"Oh no, I can tell you straight away that it's not one of ours! We don't do . . . well, poses quite like that— it would damage our high-class reputation." He turned the photograph in my hand to show me the reverse side. "Anyway, we always stamp our name and address on the back. We aren't ashamed to acknowledge our work. I suggest you try Claude Mason in Ash

Street—just along by the station."

That was the third name on my list. Murmuring thanks, I left and headed in the direction of the railway station.

The entrance to Claude Mason's studio was a doorway sandwiched between two shops, with stairs leading up. On the second floor, I entered a bright and cheerful waiting room. A woman was in there, ordering some enlargements, and Claude Mason—it had to be him—gave me a smile and waved me to a chair.

"Be with you in a second."

He was pushing forty, an ordinary-looking man who had tried to add a touch of artistic distinction with collar-length hair, a vandyked beard, a floppy bow tie, and a velvet smoking jacket in dusty purple.

He jotted down the woman's order and told her with a radiant smile that it would be ready to collect in three days' time. As she went out he turned and came toward me, his head tilted, his hands held up to frame my face judicially.

"What had you in mind, love? It's for your boy friend, I dare say? I can do you a nice six-by-eight mounted in a gilt presentation frame so he can prop you up in his bedroom."

"No . . . I'm sorry, but I just wanted some information." Again I drew the photographs from the envelope. "I was wondering if by chance you took these?"

His look of disappointment swiftly changed when he saw what I was holding out. He glanced at me closely, slyly, sizing me up.

"You know who this is, don't you? Well, of course you must, or you wouldn't be asking. I suppose you're from the press, is that it?"

"Well . . ."

Fortunately, he liked the sound of his own voice too much to wait for any more. "It shook me rigid, I can tell you, when I saw that picture of her in the paper. She's got her head screwed on all right, that one. Mind you, though, nasty business about his wife. I was reading about it this morning."

"Do you happen to know anything about her—Belle Forsyth, I mean?"

"No, love. I never set eyes on her until she walked in one morning and asked for a set of six. She said she was hoping to get some modeling work, and of course she's got the figure for it. She had everything worked out in her mind, exactly what she wanted. Not pinups, but something to turn a man on a bit, if you know what I mean." He glanced again at the prints, admiring his own professionalism. "Looks as if she won't be needing these now, though, doesn't it? Found herself a sugar daddy—that's what they used to call them. Oh well, let's hope her luck lasts through the summer."

"Is there anything else you can tell me about her? Anything at all?"

He shook his head. "I only wish there was! Be a few quid in it for me, I bet, eh? She paid cash on the nail and asked me to send her the prints in a plain envelope—very insistent about that, she was."

"Er . . . when was this, exactly?"

"Oh, it wasn't long ago. Hang on, I can tell you for sure." He flicked through the pages of his order book. "Here we are. Just four weeks yesterday."

That was all the information he could give me. I came down the steep staircase and out into the street with curiously mixed feelings. Though I'd got nothing definite, it *was* a step forward, I told myself. It was just one more indication that Brett and I were on the right track.

I arrived back at Deer's Leap in the middle of the afternoon and drove straight to the stable to garage the Rover. As I walked around to the house, I saw there was a bright orange sportscar parked by the Warrenders' entrance. Not still the press, surely?

Rudi came to the front door to meet me. He was frowning and sounded hurt.

"Why didn't you tell me you were going out, Gail? Lady Caterina said something about Seahaven."

"Yes, I did go there," I said vaguely. "Rudi, who's

that calling on the Warrenders?"

He glanced at the orange car. "Oh, that looks like Elspeth Vane's."

Surprised, I said, "Brett must have come in *her* car, then!"

I couldn't wait to tell Brett my news about the photographs of Belle. Just as I was, I went straight through to the staircase hall. Sir Ralph was standing in the telephone lobby, with the door open. He broke off his conversation and turned in my direction.

"Is that you, Gail? You'll find them in the Ivory Room."

I tapped on the door, and Caterina called to come in. "Hello, Gail dear. Did you get what you wanted in Seahaven?"

"Yes, thanks."

"Come in and sit down. Take your coat off. You do know Elspeth, don't you? I'm sure you must have met."

"Yes, we've met," said Elspeth, giving me a cool stare.

Completely at home, she was reclining gracefully on one of the settees, her long legs crossed. I saw she was fingering a small ivory carving she had taken from its place on the mantel—a twelfth-century figure of Hercules, one of Sir Ralph's most treasured pieces.

As always, Elspeth had the power to make me feel gauche and insignificant. She looked stunning in a scarlet pants suit, perfectly set off by the unobtrusive dove-gray velvet of the upholstery. Her raven hair was taken back smoothly from her forehead in a chignon. On her wrist she wore a cluster of silver bangles.

"Where's Brett?" I asked. "Did he come with you?"

Her laugh tinkled, unamused. "I thought you hadn't come bursting in just to say hello to me! No, Brett's not coming down until later. He said there was some footage he wanted to check through first. He's suddenly in a fever to start work on the Karel film again, though heaven knows why."

"It's *his* decision!" I retorted sharply.

Behind me, Sir Ralph had come into the room. He said, "Elspeth shares my opinion that completing the film is a waste of time and money. If it ever gets a television showing, which I doubt, it can only injure the career of everyone connected with it."

"I'm sure Brett knows what he's doing," I said doggedly.

"I wonder!" Elspeth's viridian green eyes held a glint of mockery, added to the cool calculation that was always there. "Brett does some very peculiar things at times. He can be an impetuous man, with sudden wild enthusiasms. Short-lived enthusiasms."

Caterina glanced unhappily from one to the other of us, sensing the electric tension but not fully understanding the cause of it.

"We must leave it to Brett," she said, in an attempt at peacemaking.

It was seven in the evening before Brett arrived. Waiting for him, never far from a window that faced the front, I heard the low snarl of his Lancia as it stormed up the last rise before Deer's Leap, then clicked down a gear to swing in at the entrance gates. His headlights sent a stream of light skittering across the hall as he came racing up the drive and slid to a stop on the sweep of gravel fronting the house. The motor was cut, the headlights snapped off, the door slammed shut, all in the space of a moment. Brett was obviously in a tearing hurry.

I opened our front door to intercept him, but he was coming to the west wing anyway, striding briskly toward me. In his hand he gripped a small tube of cardboard.

"Gail, I've got to talk to you! I've discovered something."

Behind me, the door of the Oak Room opened, and Rudi came out. He spent most of his time there now, brooding. Uselessly heaping blame on himself.

"I heard your car, Brett," he said. "Er . . . have you some news?"

"I just want a word with Gail, that's all," Brett said brusquely. He pointed to the door of the Winter Parlor. "Can we go in here, Gail?"

"Yes." Before closing the door, I glimpsed the puzzled, anxious expression on Rudi's face as he stood motionless in the hall, staring after us.

Brett dragged off his sheepskin jacket and tossed it on a chair. He began easing out the contents of the cardboard tube, all the while talking fast.

"I was planning to come back earlier, but then I decided to stay in town and have a second look at all the material we'd chucked out, in the hope that some of it might be usable after all. As it stands, the film is much too patchy, and the whole concept of the thing needs rethinking. I did find a few extra bits we could use; however, that's beside the point. What interested me was a series of stills that Eddie Fox had taken by the lake here. They're wretchedly indistinct, because there was so little light. But look at this one!"

He had unrolled a blown-up photograph and flattened it out on top of the bureau. Standing beside him, I looked at it, puzzled. Possibly, even if Brett hadn't told me, I might have recognized the lake at Deer's Leap, the conifers fringing the far bank. But I could make out little else, for the picture was foggy and blurred.

I glanced up at Brett. "I don't understand. What's so special about it?"

"It was Eddie's first attempt at photography by moonlight. He'd always felt that as the house is called Deer's Leap, it would be a pity not to include some shots of deer taken in the grounds, and Elspeth and I agreed with him. But all the time we were filming down here we never saw a sign of deer. So in the end Eddie decided he'd surprise us with some stills taken at night. He waited for the full moon, and set up an automatic camera on that ridge above the lake, timing it to take a short shot every five minutes. But when the film was processed, Eddie shoved the prints away in disgust. They were hopeless, with nothing recognizable as a deer in any of them."

The night of the full moon, Brett had said. I had a sudden memory of the silent moonlit landscape at the *mas* in Provence. It had been a half moon then, low in the sky, and on the wane.

"When were these pictures taken?" I asked him urgently. "Was it. . . ?"

He nodded. "Yes, Gail, the night Alexis disappeared. I want you to have another look. Look carefully. What do you think that is out on the lake?"

I could see only a vague gray blur. But with my eyes half closed I began to form an image that grew clearer, more definite.

"It looks like the dinghy, Brett."

"Yes, and what's in it? Or rather, who?"

It was all so indistinct. Shadowy figures with no clear outline. I said doubtfully, "That could be a woman . . . long hair . . . and the other . . . I don't know—it could be a man."

"What else do you see, Gail?"

"There seems to be a dark shape between them. It . . . it looks as if they're trying to lift it . . ." I broke off and stared at Brett, fear suddenly surging through me.

"As if they're trying to lift it over the side?" he suggested, holding my gaze intently.

I felt the muscles of my legs begin to tremble, and I gripped the hard edge of the bureau with my fingers.

"Oh, Brett, can it really be?"

"I don't see what else," he said somberly. "When you think about it, the lake at Deer's Leap would be the obvious place to dispose of a body they never expected anyone to search for."

Chapter Twenty

There was a thin mist lying low across the surface of the lake. I rowed with smooth strokes, dipping the oars carefully, feeling a curious need to preserve the silence.

From the bank Brett signaled to me with a flashlight, sweeping the light around in a counter-clockwise circle—a prearranged signal that meant I was to go more to his left.

The dinghy responded at once to my pull on the oar. As it glided on its new course, I noticed that the lights of the house, hazy through the mist, were suddenly cut off from view by a rise in the bank.

I had been astonished when Brett told me that he proposed making a dive that night.

"But you can't!" I'd protested. "I mean, not in the dark."

"There's no reason why not, Gail. The lake isn't exactly crystal clear, so I'd have to use an underwater flashlight whether it was night or day. I've got to go down at once. I couldn't sleep not knowing whether Alexis is down there or not. And neither could you!"

Brett was right, of course. But I was frightened for his safety.

"Don't you need all sorts of elaborate equipment?"

"I've got an aqualung and all the rest of the gear out in the car. I borrowed it from a club I belong to. You don't have to worry, Gail. I've done a fair bit of scuba diving in my time."

Brett had slipped through to the main wing of the house to make some excuse to Caterina about us not joining them for dinner. I don't know quite what he told her. I guessed that Elspeth wouldn't be pleased. While he was gone I sped upstairs and dressed myself in the thickest pair of slacks I possessed, a chunky sweater, and a quilted anorak jacket.

Rudi wasn't anywhere around when I came down again. As soon as Brett got back, we went outside and collected the diving equipment from the rear seat of the Lancia. Brett carried the aqualung cylinder itself, the life jacket, and various bits and pieces. I took the pack containing the "wet suit," which was bulky but not heavy.

"I'll need to wear the full gear for warmth," he said. "This time of year a spring-fed lake is going to be mighty cold."

At the lakeside we had righted the dinghy, and I climbed in. Brett shoved me afloat, and then, taking the flashlight with him, he started clambering through the tangled mass of dead bracken on the bank up to the point where Eddie Fox had set up his camera. By comparing the photograph with the actual scene, looking at the lake from the same angle, Brett had decided he could guide me fairly accurately to the right spot.

He was signaling to me again now, a series of short flashes, which indicated that I was to go out toward the middle. After a moment, the light was waved in a clockwise direction. Responding, I edged a little to the right.

The light went out. Brett reckoned I was now in position. I fumbled around at my feet and found the small marking buoy made of bright-orange plastic and dropped it over the side.

By the time I had rowed back to the little pebble beach, Brett had already thrown off his clothes and was climbing into the skin-tight wet suit. Slipping his arms through the harness, he heaved the aqualung cylinder onto his back. Then he put on the inflatable lifejacket. He tossed the pair of fins into the dinghy.

"All set now!"

It was difficult for me to keep the boat steady while Brett climbed in. I followed him, pushing off with an oar and rowing toward the center of the lake once more. When we judged ourselves in about the right position, Brett shined the bright beam across the water while I slued the boat around, scanning a wide semi-circle, searching for the orange ball floating on the surface.

"There it is!" said Brett. "Ease her over a bit, Gail —that's right."

Brett had pulled the rubber fins onto his feet. He made some final small adjustments, then sat up on the end board in the stern, facing me, ready to dive. Silhouetted against the whiteness of the mist, he looked a strange, almost monstrous figure.

"Here goes, then," he said. "Wish me luck."

"Luck . . . ?"

"It's what we want to find, Gail—what we've *got* to find. We know—both of us—that no amount of wishing will ever bring Alexis back to life."

His hand went up to his face, fixing the mouthpiece, holding the mask in place. He rolled slowly backward, overbalancing and hitting the water with a splash that seemed to tear the night apart. Suddenly freed of his weight, the dinghy bobbed wildly. I steadied it, gripping the sides with my hands, and stared down into the dark water. For a few moments I could see a glow of yellowish, brownish light. But swiftly it faded until I could detect nothing.

The boat's dancing motion grew less, and soon it was quite still again, the surface of the lake barely rippling. I could hear a curious faint plopping noise, and at first I was puzzled. Then I knew what it was—a stream of tiny bubbles rushing to the surface, the air that Brett was breathing out.

A plane droned faintly overhead, lost in the vastness of the sky. Across the surface of the water the mist was drifting sluggishly in some unfelt wind, curling into mysterious white wraiths that seemed about to engulf me. But my thoughts were concentrated on what was happening below me. Somewhere down there Brett was moving slowly on the bottom of the lake, groping his way, searching the mud-stirred depths with his flashlight.

Minutes crept past. The soda stream of air bubbles breaking on the surface was my only contact with Brett. But somehow I couldn't feel it as a contact. It was too unreal, too remote to have any meaning.

Yet if it were to stop!

I had never, ever, known time to drag as it did now. Though I knew that in truth it was only minutes, to me the wait seemed unending.

Peering down, trying to pierce the secret darkness of the water, my eyes began to play tricks. Could I really see something, or was it just my wishful imagination?

After another long age I felt certain I could detect the faintest paling, a lessening of the utter black opacity. Very slowly, the glimmer grew stronger, more definite, until I could see the round yellow disk of the flashlight itself.

Suddenly, five yards away from me, Brett broke to the surface in a quick swirl of water. He looked around him, saw where I was, and swam over. Grabbing the side of the dinghy with one hand, he slipped out his mouthpiece and lifted the mask.

The beam of the flashlight shone up into the sky, but in the light scattered by the mist, I could see Brett's face, a circle of white in the black rubber hood.

I waited fearfully, unable to voice the question.

He said at last, "Yes, Gail."

Even now, something within me wanted to reject the dreadful knowledge.

"You're . . . you're sure it *is* Alexis?" I faltered. "Really sure?"

"Who else?" said Brett wearily. "A body, wrapped in some sort of canvas, weighted down, at this exact spot. Who else could it be, Gail?"

There were things to be done now, and that saved me from breaking down. First I had to help Brett back into the boat. He unclipped the harness, and I knelt and took the heavy aqualung cylinder off his back, then helped him as he heaved himself over the stern, clumsy and awkward in the slippery rubber suit.

"Row straight back. There's a good girl. We'll leave the buoy to mark the spot. I've got to get out of these things. I'm freezing!"

Chapter Twenty-One

In my bedroom, the room that had been mine since I was a girl of thirteen, I wandered around touching things, trying to find comfort in fingering my childish

treasures. There was the collection of china dogs that
Alexis and I had added to whenever we came across
one with a suitably appealing face; the little mother-
of pearl jewel box that had been a birthday present
from Madeleine; a serpent-shaped piece of driftwood
brought back from an outing to the sea on one of Madeleine's good days.

Brett, at this moment, was on his way to London.

When we returned from the lake, Brett had sent
Jenny to fetch his father from the dining room. Sir
Ralph came at once, his table napkin still in his hand.

"We'd better go to the library," he said. "Gail, are
you here too?"

"Yes, Sir Ralph."

Long familiar with every room at Deer's Leap, he
walked with unhesitating steps across to the fireplace,
where a bright coal fire burned. He turned and faced
us.

"Jenny said it was something very important."

Brett told his father everything, as briefly as such a
story could be told. I had to admire Sir Ralph's self-
control. His blind face registered his emotions—astonishment, horror, grief—but he allowed Brett to finish
without interruption. I pitied him. Years seemed to
have been added to his age in the space of a few minutes.

"Why didn't you tell me about this before, Brett?"
he said at last in a quiet voice.

"Because we couldn't be certain until we had some
sort of proof. It wouldn't have been fair to worry you."

There was an uneasy pause. Then Sir Ralph muttered, "You mean you were afraid I might not believe
you! Perhaps you were right, Brett. It's an incredible
story."

"The question is, Father, what do we do now?
Ought we to contact the Intelligence people rather
than the police? It's possible they might want to keep
quiet about the discovery of Alexis's body and give
themselves a better chance to track down some of the
people involved."

Sir Ralph nodded. "I think you may be right. I have contacts, of course. Do you want me to call someone now to put things in motion?"

"It might be risky to use the phone. When you remember how thorough the Communists are, there's quite a possibility the lines here are being tapped. It would explain how they got on so quickly to the fact that Gail was going to Majorca. She rang the airport to book her flight."

So in the end it was decided that Brett should drive at once to London to see a man Sir Ralph had known for many years.

Brett came and put his hands on my shoulders. "I may be very late getting back, Gail, so try and get some rest. I promise to come and wake you at once." To his father he said, "How much will you tell Caterina?"

Sir Ralph hesitated. "Nothing, I think—for the moment. Tomorrow I suppose I shall have to."

For a while after the sound of Brett's Lancia had faded into the night, his father and I remained in the library. We were silent, both of us deep in our thoughts. At length Sir Ralph lifted his head, clearing his throat huskily.

"I cannot tell you how deeply I regret the harsh things I have said and thought about your uncle in these past days. He was my friend, and I should have had more faith. Unfortunately, unforgivably, I allowed myself to be deceived by appearances." He turned his head away for a moment, then faced me again. "Gail, my dear, you know, don't you, that Alexis would not have cared about death so long as the ideals he stood for survived? And now, when the world learns the truth, his books will be read, his teachings remembered. With ten times the force!" He gave a deep sigh. "Poor Madeleine—at least her sufferings are over now. Without Alexis, life would have had no meaning for her."

I wanted to answer him, but I could not find my voice. He reached out a hand to me, and I put mine

into it, feeling his fingers tighten. I knew that in his
blindness Sir Ralph too was in need of this physical
expression of sympathy.

After a long silence, he suggested that perhaps we
ought to join Caterina and Elspeth. But I didn't feel up
to facing them this evening. Particularly Elspeth. So I
said I was rather tired and would prefer to return to
the west wing.

I intended telling Rudi at once about our discovery
in the lake. But he was nowhere around, not in the
Oak Room or anywhere else downstairs. Either he was
up in his bedroom, or he'd gone out to get some air.
Perhaps it was just as well, I thought with relief. I felt
utterly drained, emotionally exhausted. I went up to
my room and closed the door, thankful to be alone for
a little while.

I kept my ears tuned to the stillness and silence of
the house. When, presently, I heard the door of the
Oak Room beneath me being opened, I braced myself
to go down. I dreaded the task of breaking the news to
Rudi, but I could not shirk it.

At the turn of the stairs I paused, hearing a voice.
Not Rudi's but Freda Aiken's. A few steps nearer, and
I realized that she was talking on the phone. The study
door was slightly ajar, and though her voice was low,
I caught the words distinctly.

"I tell you that they know!"

I froze at the foot of the staircase. More than what
she said, it was the tone of her voice that arrested me.
There was panic in it, a sort of desperation.

She was listening now to someone who spoke at
length. I crept a few paces closer, standing behind the
door.

Freda said in a cracked whisper, "But it was nothing *I* did! The girl realized it wasn't her uncle she saw
in Geneva. I heard her telling Rudi Bruckner. And
then tonight she and Warrender were out on the lake
in a boat. He had diving equipment and went down.
They must have found the body."

She paused again, and above the furious thudding of

my own heartbeat, I fancied I could hear the voice at the other end—a man's voice, charged with anger.

"You can't blame *me!*" exclaimed Freda suddenly. "It was nothing *I* did." Another pause, then hurriedly: "Yes, Bruckner's outside somewhere. I saw him go. And she's next door with the Warrenders at the moment. That's why I took the chance to phone you. But I mustn't be long. . . . Yes . . . yes, I understand. I'll leave at once—right away."

I heard her replace the telephone, and I quickly slipped through the open door of the Winter Parlor, out of sight. I heard the study light switched off, the door closed. Swiftly, Freda crossed to the stairs and went up, making for her bedroom.

I was too shocked and stunned to move. It hadn't occurred to me that anyone else in the house could be involved now that Belle Forsyth was gone. Her unspeakable job had been completed, and Alexis was dead and discredited. What possible reason could the Communists have for placing another agent at Deer's Leap? What had remained still to be done?

Madeleine!

My entire body went ice-cold. I began to shake, powerless to control the wild trembling of my legs, the sickness in my stomach, the crawling of my skin.

My aunt's death had been the final condemnation of Alexis Karel. If anybody still doubted that he had behaved despicably, this act of desperation on the part of his heartbroken, invalid wife would have convinced them. Everyone the world over must be thinking now that he had as good as killed his wife with his own two hands.

Had such a convenient and superbly timed piece of propaganda really been pure chance? Or had the Communists contrived that, too?

I thought about the tragedy I had witnessed from the garden. Could it be that Madeleine had been fighting desperately with Freda in order to *save* her life and not to *end* it?

I closed my eyes, seeing it all again, reliving those

horrifying moments. The flutter of white inside the room, then Madeleine at the window, calling, calling Alexis's name. And Freda Aiken coming up behind her, holding her, pulling her back. *Or pushing her!* With so frail an opponent as Madeleine, it would be easy to make the one look like the other.

If Freda had told her that Alexis was out there in the grounds, it would have been enough to send Madeleine rushing impetuously to the window, calling his name. And afterward, the discovery of the newspaper in her room would account for her "suicide."

If only Brett were here, I thought frantically. But he was halfway to London by now. Sir Ralph, being blind, could do little to help. Caterina and Elspeth hadn't the least idea what was going on, and it would take too long to explain.

I had to find Rudi.

I'd heard Freda Aiken say on the phone that he was outside somewhere. I opened the French windows and slipped out to the terrace. Swiftly, I circled the house, then ran across to the stable. But there was no sign of him anywhere.

I dared not call out for fear of alerting Freda. I sped down the path to the lake, stumbling in the darkness, whispering Rudi's name. But no answer came. In desperation, I turned and ran back toward the house. The light in Freda Aiken's room, her shadow moving behind the curtain, seemed to draw me, making me hurry faster. *I'll leave right away,* she had said. She must be stopped!

I went back in through the French windows and ran straight upstairs to Freda's room. I burst open the door.

She was standing at the wardrobe, taking down hangers. A suitcase lay open on the bed, already half filled. The drawers of the dressing table were open, too.

She spun around and her face went pale.

"Oh, Miss Fleming—you did startle me! I didn't know you were in this side of the house." Already she was recovering, getting back to the pose of pathetic gratitude she had adopted since Madeleine's death. "Actually . . . well, to tell you the truth, I was thinking about your kindness in letting me stay on, but it doesn't really seem fair to have asked you. I was going to move out in the morning, find a room somewhere."

"You . . . you killed Madeleine!" I said chokily.

Her eyes narrowed, going wary. The dress she was holding slipped through her fingers to the floor.

"Whatever are you saying, Miss Fleming? It's dreadful to talk like that! I admit I feel to blame for not watching your aunt more carefully, but that doesn't give you the right to accuse me of—"

"You killed her!" I repeated. "You killed her because that's what you were sent here to do. I heard what you said on the phone just now."

"You heard!" she gasped. "Oh dear! I thought you were safely next door with the Warrenders."

Casually she started edging toward me. I stood my ground, defying her. But then, before I realized what she meant to do, she lunged forward and swiftly turned the key in the lock. Slipping it into the pocket of her cardigan, she stood and smiled at me maliciously. "There now! We can have a cozy chat while I finish my packing."

I boiled with anger—at letting myself be duped by her, at being so impotent.

"I don't know what you hope to achieve," I said icily. "I'm not frail like my aunt, so you're not going to push me out of the window."

She bent and picked up the dress she had dropped and started to fold it, slowly and deliberately.

"There will be no need for such drastic measures, Miss Fleming. I've got some very effective knock-out shots that will put you out cold for a couple of hours or so and no more than a nasty headache when you wake up again. By then I shall be well away from here."

"You don't think I'm going to let you give me an injection of dope."

"I was trained in a very tough school," she said

scornfully. "There are precious few *men* who could get the better of me."

I believed her. I could sense a sort of brute strength in that short, squat figure. I put on an act of false confidence because there was nothing else I could do.

"You seem to forget there are other people in the house. Rudi is just downstairs."

"Is he? And have you told him about what you heard me saying on the phone?"

"Naturally! If I'm not down again in a minute or two, he'll be coming up."

That didn't have the effect I'd hoped for. Freda merely shrugged carelessly. "I'll deal with Rudi Bruckner later, after I've seen to you!"

She went to a drawer of the dressing table, and I watched her take out a tiny syringe. Rapidly, I scanned the room for something small and heavy and spotted a pair of Freda's stout walking shoes beside the bed. In a sudden swift movement I dived for one of them and ran with it to the window. Dragging aside the curtain I smashed the heel into the casement, once and then again. The lead bent and buckled, and a dozen diamond panes shattered and fell tinkling to the paved terrace below. Surely that would attract attention. If Rudi was somewhere outside, he must have heard it.

Before I could start shouting for help, I saw Freda coming at me. I dodged aside, so that she fell against the window. Flinging up a hand to save her balance, she cut her wrist on a jagged edge of glass. Blood oozed and she gripped the wound, cursing.

Her momentary distraction was my opportunity. Grasping the full-length chintz curtains, I tugged at them so that the fittings gave way and the whole lot came crashing down. The heavy brass rod caught the side of Freda's head, and she must have been slightly stunned. I grasped up an armful of the fabric and flung it over her, enveloping her in clinging folds.

In an instant I had snatched the door key from her cardigan pocket and was running across the room. The lock clicked back smoothly, and as I opened the door

I plucked the key out again, intending to lock Freda inside. But I wasn't spared time enough for that. Even as I pulled the door closed after me, Freda was already there, dragging it open. I felt her tremendous strength, the strength of a man.

I let go and ran for the stairs. But, fatally, I turned right as though from my own room, instead of turning left. Ahead of me, through a curtained archway, were the stairs to the attics. I raced up them in the dark with no clear idea in my mind except to get away from Freda. I recalled from my childhood explorations that at the end of the attic corridor there was a little cubbyhole under the eaves. I sped along to it and crawled inside.

I could hear Freda blundering up the unfamiliar stairs. At the top she paused, and then after a moment she found the light switch. But my hiding place was shadowed by a heavy beam of the roof.

Slowly, Freda came along the corridor, flinging open the door of each room as she reached it, peering inside, satisfying herself it was empty before moving on. All the time she was getting nearer.

There was a cold draft blowing down the nape of my neck, and that brought back a memory. I was about fourteen the first time I had found this place, found the sloping skylight that led out onto the jumbled rooftops of Deer's Leap. I'd been out there a few times, unknown to Alexis, who would probably have had a fit if he'd found out about it.

Carefully, I felt for the remembered catch. I turned it, and silently, inch by inch, I eased up the heavy glazed door. But when I'd got it wide open, it suddenly slipped from my nervous fingers and fell backward onto the roof with a crash of splintering glass and tiles.

I froze and heard Freda Aiken's exclamation, her footsteps running along the corridor. In a quick movement I heaved myself through the opening and out onto the roof.

What now? Useless to try and close the door—it couldn't be fastened from the outside. I slithered the couple of feet down the steep-angled roof to the lead gully I knew was there, hearing the loosened tiles sliding with me. I followed the gully to where it disgorged into a water spout at the front of the house. Between the crenellated parapet wall and the pitch of the roof there was a narrow channel. I began to edge my way along, with the idea that when I reached the point above the great porch, a drop of about ten feet would take me to another skylight that might with luck be unlocked, or that I could smash.

I knew that Freda Aiken had climbed out through the skylight after me, and she must have taken some other route across the hodgepodge of roofs. She suddenly appeared ahead of me, outlined against the sky. In the faint starlight we crouched and stared at each other.

"Why not be sensible?" she said in a conversational tone. "I'm not going to hurt you—just give you a little injection. I've got the stuff right here. It will put you out for long enough for me to get well clear."

"You'll never get away," I said. "Rudi will—"

"You can forget about Rudi Bruckner. He'll do exactly what he's told—just as he's done in the past."

Rudi! A terrible wave of darkness swept over me, a sense of utter hopelessness.

"It was lucky for us, having Bruckner so well dug in with your uncle. It enabled us to get Belle Forsyth fixed up with a job here without any trouble. And then me!"

"But Rudi would never do anything to harm Alexis," I said huskily. "I'm sure he wouldn't."

"I think you're right," she acknowledged. "But he's a very credulous young man. He actually believed that Alexis Karel had run off with Belle, because she had encouraged him to think they were having an affair. If he had known the truth—that we had killed Alexis Karel that night, and substituted a double in his place —he might have been more difficult to handle. But it's too late for him to do anything about it. You see, he has a sister living in Czechoslovakia. Need I say more?"

I tried to blot out my misery, concentrating only on the need to get away from Freda, to raise the alarm, to prevent her escaping. In a daze I began to edge back the way I had come, thinking I might reach the skylight before she caught up with me. Stumbling against the parapet, I felt it tremble, and suddenly it gave way. Just in time I flung myself flat against the tiles of the steep-pitched roof, clinging there spread-eagled. Thirty feet below me I heard the heavy stonework crash onto the gravel.

Even Freda Aiken was startled for a moment. Then she laughed. "You are in a tricky situation now, aren't you? Pity you didn't go down with that chunk of parapet. Still, we can soon fix that. Just a little push . . ."

She started inching her way toward me. I tried to shift my position slightly and immediately felt myself sliding down to the very edge of the roof. My foot dislodged more of the crumbling stonework and sent it plunging.

There was another noise from above us, someone frantically scrambling over the tiles. A dark figure appeared on the ridge above my head.

"Gail, are you all right?" It was Rudi's voice, hoarse with fear. "You're not hurt?"

Before I could answer, Freda called up to him. "You arrived just in the nick of time. Go and get the car out for me. If you behave yourself, I'll take you with me. Otherwise, you'll have a hell of a lot of explaining to do."

Rudi ignored her. "Gail, you *are* all right, aren't you? Tell me."

"Yes, but I'm stuck. I dare not move an inch."

"Then keep still! Stay just where you are, and I'll come."

Freda warned him in a dangerous voice, "Don't bother about her, just do as I tell you."

"I've finished taking orders from you! I wish I'd had the courage to stand up to you long ago."

"Really!" she said mockingly. "I thought you were devoted to the big sister who brought you up. If you don't do what you're told, Rudi Bruckner, it's going to be too bad for her!"

Again Rudi ignored Freda and spoke to me, his voice imploring. "Gail, please try to understand. I didn't want to help them, but I *had* to. They kept threatening what they'd do to Bozena and her family if I didn't carry out their instructions. But even so, if I'd realized what they were planning . . . I just thought they wanted to plant Belle here as a sort of spy, and I didn't see how there could be much harm in that. And then . . . then I really believed that Alexis had let her seduce him. I ought to have known him better."

From across the rooftops I heard my name called. It was Sir Ralph's voice.

"Gail! What's going on up here? I heard breaking glass, and then a lot of masonry falling."

"Get help, Sir Ralph," I called back frantically. "It's Freda Aiken. She's trying to kill me."

To my horror, I realized that Sir Ralph, too, had climbed out through the skylight and was fumbling his way along. A blind man!

"No, Sir Ralph, go back! Go and get help."

But he still came on. Fearfully, I twisted my head and saw his shadowy figure appear where the gully ended.

"Where are you, Gail?"

He edged toward me, his hand on the parapet, using it as a guide and support. A step or two farther and he would reach the point where the parapet wall was broken away. There would be nothing to stop him falling.

I screamed out, "Stay where you are, Sir Ralph. Don't move! For God's sake!"

This time my urgency got through to him. He stood quite still. No one spoke a word.

Four people, all of us frozen like figures in stone. I was stretched out on the steeply sloping tiles, clinging for my life; Rudi straddled the ridge ten feet above me, too far away to help. Freda Aiken, still with solid parapet to support her, could edge along and send me crashing to the gravel court below. And—if she wanted

—the sightless, bewildered Sir Ralph, too.

In the taut silence a sound penetrated through my fear. Faint, far off, the familiar throaty boom of an exhaust. Brett's Lancia! But it wasn't possible. Brett was on his way to London, miles and miles away from here.

Nearby, I heard the scrape of a shifting tile and realized it was Freda, starting to move along to me.

"If you'd had any sense, Gail Fleming," she said, "you'd have been lying peacefully unconscious on my bed at this moment, while I made a quiet getaway. As it is, I'll have to deal with you another way."

Imperatively, Rudi called,. "You stay where you are! Leave Gail alone!"

But she still came on, one step at a time.

"Whatever is happening?" cried Sir Ralph. "If only I could see!"

Freda was scarcely a yard from me, near enough for her outstretched hand to reach me, to give me a push. I braced myself to fight her off, knowing I hardly stood a chance because the least movement would send me sliding, slithering helplessly off the roof.

In those final split seconds I heard the car again, being driven hard. This time I knew for sure that it was Brett.

And then there was another sound, a sudden wild cry, weird and scarcely human. Then a clattering, splintering noise of roof tiles breaking and slipping, almost as if the whole house was collapsing under us. Rudi's dark form hurtled past me down the steep-angled pitch of the roof. With another yell, he smashed into Freda Aiken, carrying her and himself and more of the stone parapet over the edge and out into space.

I closed my eyes as I heard the terrible screams and thuds of bodies and masonry plunging down and crashing to the gravel far below.

And when that dreadful sound was over, I heard the Lancia racing up the drive.

Caterina had a bedroom made ready for me, for I could not have returned to the west wing that night.

But it was almost dawn before any of us got to bed.

The police were at Deer's Leap again, all over the house. And other men who were not police, grim-faced men who asked a different set of questions, issued curt instructions, kept the press at bay.

I told them my story, over and over, until at last Brett protested, "For heaven's sake, can't you let Miss Fleming rest? She's had enough."

"I don't mind, Brett—if it helps."

And so once again, right from the beginning to the end. To the final moment when Brett, after guiding his father back to a secure position, had come climbing over the rooftops to me, ripping out tiles to give him footholds on the timber framework beneath.

He held me for a moment, murmuring reassurances. Then slowly we made our way back along the gully and through the skylight into the house.

"Brett, what was it made you turn back home?" I asked him breathlessly. "However did you guess?"

"Leave it now, Gail. I'll explain later."

Freda Aiken and Rudi were both dead. Killed instantly, just as Madeleine had been.

"Rudi did it to save my life, Brett," I said with an aching sadness. "He didn't have to—if he'd let Freda kill me, nobody would have known for sure how it happened. Your father couldn't see."

"Perhaps," said Brett quietly, "the poor devil knew he'd reached the end of the road and was trying to square the account. Besides, Rudi was in love with you. I've always known that."

Again I asked Brett what had made him turn around and come back to Deer's Leap.

"Something was niggling at the back of my mind—all the time I was driving. I knew there was some inconsistency somewhere. And then it suddenly hit me. Do you remember Rudi telling us that when Belle first came to work here, back in April, he was bogged down with the indexing of Alexis's book?"

"Yes, but what . . . ?"

"He was lying, Gail. He was trying to cover up for not being able to give us the details about Belle, and in doing so he said too much. I suddenly remembered a conversation I'd had with Alexis one time. He was talking about Rudi, praising him to the skies, and he mentioned how Rudi had even given up his holiday in order to do the indexing. His holiday in *August*. That was enough for me. I knew then that Rudi was deliberately concealing something, that somehow or other he was involved in all this. At once I turned the car around and headed back to Deer's Leap. Even so, I'd still not have been in time if Rudi hadn't . . ."

In the morning Alexis's body was raised by divers from the bottom of the lake. Brett and I stood watching silently from the bank. When we returned to the house, Elspeth had left, which was a great relief to me. Brett explained that she had gone back to do some work on the film, and that he wanted to drive me to London next afternoon to see a run-through.

"Of course, there will have to be some final editing and polishing," he said, "but I've decided, after all, to show it in an unfinished state—without any additional material except the commentary. Everyone will understand just why the film was never finished—because Alexis Karel was murdered in a Communist plot to discredit his name."

In the private projection suite at the TV studios a small group was gathered. Elspeth was there with the rest of Brett's team, and a few other people I hadn't met before.

It was a deeply moving experience to see my uncle on the screen against the familiar background of Deer's Leap, to hear again his vibrant, living voice. Madeleine appeared, too, looking fraily beautiful, and their devotion to one another came across unmistakably. The final sequence of the film showed Alexis at his desk in the Oak Room, reminiscing about his homeland. There was no bitterness in his words, and his last message was one of optimism and hope.

When it was over, I felt in no mood to stay around and chat. Brett understood. We left the studio at once, and he took me up in the lift to the roof of the building, where we stood leaning against the balustrade, staring out across the hazy expanse of London on a winter afternoon.

"It was a wonderful film," I said at length, my voice still tight with emotion. "A wonderful tribute to Alexis. Thank you, Brett."

He nodded. "I'm glad you liked it." There was silence again, then Brett went on, "Gail, I . . . I want to explain about Elspeth and me."

"I know about Elspeth and you," I said bleakly.

"But you don't, darling! You never have understood. That night, the night you phoned me at the hotel in Manchester and she answered—it wasn't what you thought. Elspeth was in my room for no other reason than to discuss the film we were working on."

"Was she?" I heard myself saying. "I wonder if Elspeth would agree with that."

Brett caught his breath impatiently. "Gail, I know this isn't the moment to be rough with you, but will you please accept once and for all that it's you I care about. Just you! And now, for God's sake, let's forget about Elspeth."

"I'll try, Brett," I murmured. And suddenly it struck me that it wasn't going to take all that much effort to forget her. I hadn't anything to fear now from Elspeth Vane. Perhaps I never had.